LOVERS LIVING
LOVERS DEAD

NOVELS BY RICHARD LORTZ

Bereavements
A Crowd of Voices
Lovers Living, Lovers Dead
The Valdepeñas
Dracula's Children

LOVERS LIVING
LOVERS DEAD

RICHARD LORTZ

Second Chance Press
Sagaponack, New York

Jay Landesman Limited
London

Originally published in the United States 1977 by
G.P. Putnam's Sons, New York.

First republication 1981 by Second Chance Press,
Sagaponack, New York.

First published 1981 in Great Britain by
Jay Landesman Limited, London.

Library of Congress Catalogue Card Number: 81-80896
International Standard Book Numbers:
    (U.S.) 0-933256-28-0 (Clothbound)
          0-933256-29-9 (Paperbound)
    (U.K.) 0-905150-35-X

Printed in the United States of America

For Ramon:
departure in a new affection

On our stage, at the intersection of ten partitions set up between the gallery and the footlights, comedy and ancient terror pursue their harmonies and divide their idylls.

The Starlings

*All the women he had ever known were assassinated;
what havoc in the garden! At the point of the sword
they blessed him. He never ordered new ones. Wom-
en reappeared.*

*After the hunt or the libations, he killed everyone
who followed him. Everyone followed him.*

*He entertained himself with the torture of rare ani-
mals. He set palaces aflame. He rushed into crowds
and slaughtered all who were near him. Yet throngs,
gilded roofs, beautiful animals remained.*

ONE

IT WAS THAT TIME OF SPRING: when, indeed, memory mixed with desire and bred lilacs out of the dead land.

But it brought the starlings, too; *they* were back—for the *third* time, and watching a great dark cloud of them cluster far above her like a plague of locusts, blackening the sun, Christine was touched with a now-familiar wonder and panic.

She'd come out into the garden in the late summer-warm afternoon wearing one of her old maternity dresses: the crushed crinkly gold she used to wear to faculty teas. Underneath, placed very low on the abdomen, as if "the baby" were hourly imminent, she'd tied a small round pillow on which was painted a crude, childlike face.

She'd made up her eyes the way she thought Nefertiti might have looked: almond and angular, and wore every bit of junk jewelry she owned—all this being a kind of dress rehearsal for a little comedy-drama, like so many she played, to amuse her husband, Michael, if he was so inclined, though more often than not lately, she succeeded in entertaining only herself, and sometimes the children if they happened to be near.

The moment she heard his car crunching the stones in the driveway, she'd planned to call from the highest window in the house—the round, spooky one in the attic room beneath the gabled roof where she kept her trunk: "Michael, go to the summerhouse; you'll find a pitcher of lemonade and some iced cookies."

Then, after he'd seated himself amid his sundry portfolios and blue pencils and Comparative Literature II midterm test papers—or was it French English this week?—*she* would appear: all spangled and goldly pregnant, to confound him with eyes that were ancient history and the shock of an instant baby. So blessed, all that fretful, pointless worry would leave his haunted eyes, and when he threw back his handsome head, laughing, she'd look quickly into his empty mouth and count every gold filling he owned, knowing their *exact* number, once and for all.

But the starlings were about to ruin both drama and joke, and as they swirled closer, threatening, they were of much more interest and importance than the strategy of counting Michael's fillings, or the Egyptian baby she'd planned to have, popping it out before him from between her legs like a bubble of bubblegum.

She watched intently as they patterned themselves into a narrow black cone, then flattened out, fanshaped, and with a vast hollow roar of wings and wind and muted hacking cries, descended, as they had twice before, into the giant dead oak at the end of the garden, the one that all winter, Michael kept saying over and over simply *had*

to come down, no matter what the expense, else it might
fall and someone get hurt.

Instantly, before her astonished eyes, the oak again became a "starling tree," every empty space of it, all its leaf-
bare twigs and branches that were blistered with rot and
flowers of fungus, so blackly crowded and stuck together
it looked as if God's sticky fingers had emptied out a box-
ful of raisins—until one saw how it *breathed*: all of it
alive, trembling with glossy feathers, scaly claws, and a
guerrilla army of glinting watchful eyes.

Looking at the teeming, writhing cluster—enough to
have eclipsed the sun—Christine found it as intolerable
as before. Loathsome. Repellent. But quite as fascinating: indeed, irresistible, and as she advanced toward the
tree, step by cautious step—believing the birds dangerous, capable of violence and injury— a cacaphony of
noisy, noisome croaks and chirps and chatterings became
gradually still, hushed and waiting.

It was happening for the third time!—and Christine's
skin began to crawl.

He had separated himself from the rest—bigger than
most, and almost inky black; not a starling at all, possibly
a raven, a crow; whatever he was, he dropped to the foot
of the tree in one gentle, graceful swoop, and turning his
head, fastened a glassy eye on hers.

And there he stood, with so much presence and pride,
such styilzed posture, she suspected he was "titled"—
and had to strain her chest to keep from laughing out
loud at the thought, hating him intensely, yet, inexplicably, loving him too—this bold *official*, this pompous
spokesman, preposterous *prince* of all the others now beginning to cacker and caw behind him: the yeas and nays
of a teeming treeful of motely citizens and senators.

Astonishingly, he was ringed!—she had not noticed it

before: he wore a tiny gold band above one spidery claw. So apparently he had been *owned* at one time!—and taught his familiar ways and strange tricks. What else could she call them? Perhaps the pathetic creature had performed professionally—on a stage, or before cameras—owned by a dwarf and chained to a stick!—able to move only a foot this way and that, backward and forward, toward her and away—as he was doing now, ostensibly for her pleasure but actually for the reward he must expect: the bit of raw meat, the sliver of writhing worm popped into his mouth. Ah, it must be so: the pink toothless cavity between the sharp bones of his beak was gaping.

He puffed out the feathers of his chest until he appeared twice his size, wings fluttering, small twin clouds of dust rising as the quivered tips beat the dead gray soil between the immense rotted roots of the tree.

A few queer foot movements followed: the tiny knot of a knee bending a thread-thin splinter of a leg in a gesture that looked absurdly like the Pope's blessing!

Every movement was bilateral: what the left leg did, the right did also. Next, four fingerlike talons took turns raking the air, quite as if to seize the hem of her golden dress; then, abruptly, desisted. With a last violent shake of head and tail, the bird became motionless, the eyes partly filmed, half-lidded, but still staring—so it seemed—directly into hers. Oh!—it was too hideous and laughable to bear!

Even on a stick, on a stage, before cameras—with a painted dwarf to prod him, and a golden chain to keep him from flying away—*who* would be entertained by *that?!*

What the bird was doing, of course, was sexual. It was

the mating dance of the starling, or the crow, or the raven—whatever he was. And when Christine suddenly realized it, it was with such a startled intake and expulsion of breath that the pillow slipped and dropped from her abdomen to her feet. She stumbled backward, tripping over her skirt, and *there* was the Egyptian baby, born before its time, grinning up at her, while, in an effort to keep her balance and not fall, her arms flew upward and out in a violent gesture.

Whether it was simply the violence of the gesture or that her suitor considered himself rejected, she never knew—only the wrath of the others, the pandemonium that followed. A starburst of birds. They so inundated her that for a moment she thought they would surely bear her away, like an army of ants sweeping along a carcass a thousand times their size.

Two of them hit her forehead so forcibly they lay instantly dead, or unconscious, at her feet. Others nipped and fretted, pulled strands of her hair, their thin cries so multiple and magnified she covered her ears. One got caught beneath her skirt and she shrieked as she felt the piercing track of its claws move up her leg. With a fist she beat it to a wet pulp against tightened thigh muscles.

Disheveled, distraught, weeping, afraid, her lovely dress torn and stained with blood, her "baby" dead—*aborted,* lying soiled in the dust and the incredible ruins of the afternoon, Christine went straight to the house and up to the attic, opened her trunk and returned with a shotgun almost as big as herself.

Once more they had reassembled in their vast, black, churning cluster in the tree, quite as before, stupid and memoryless, not knowing what they'd done, frozen in instinct, in behavior as rigid, as unyielding as an exoskele-

ton: all squawking beak and glittering eye, feathers
preened, ticks eaten, itches scratched, and the whole of
the tree's massive trunk spotted, half white-washed with
a constant shower of their chalky ooze.

An abomination.

As a child, she had many times gone hunting with her
father: to watch him kill, see the animals strung up and
disemboweled, stripped of their skin; once she had seen
seven perfect babies tumble out of a lioness as a Ujaki
tribesman ripped open its belly with a great curved *ciizk*.

When she was old enough and sufficiently strong to
manage its weight and not flounder behind the impact of
its recoil, she'd learned how to use a rifle herself, and to
use it well. Later, under her father's fanatic tutelage she
became expert in the use of most any firearm.

Now memory served, if a bit hazily, since it had been
so long since she'd handled a shotgun. It was a weapon
held in low esteem, useless for hunting big game, but
packing the power and shock of a hand grenade, unsur-
passed in an emergency, ever ready to bring down a tiger
as it crouched to spring, even to stop or divert the charge
of a raging rhino.

So although her knowledge of the gun was meagre and
basic, what she remembered was enough: how to "break"
it in half—over a knee at the moment because it was thoroughly rusted—and insert two of the giant red shells.

The closer she came to the starlings, the more agitated
they became, as if, instinct be damned, they suspected
her purpose and knew the meaning of the long, ugly,
double-mouthed snout she was pointing toward the very
heart of their nest. Several of them fluttered away but
came instantly back, unable to resist the collective mind
that demanded that all of them roost, while the din of

them swelled to such dissonance and shrillness Christine feared her eardrums might burst.

She took wavering aim, one eye screwed shut, the other a slit of narrowed concentration.

The exact second her finger tightened on the trigger, she heard the crunch of stones in the driveway and knew it was Michael.

But the tree had already exploded!—an instant mandala of fire so swift, intricate and vast she felt like a saint struck dead by the sight of God's face. Her legs buckled, her body rose from the ground like a flying aerialist, to be flung back in a smothering rain of blood, feathers and shattered entrails.

Many of the birds weren't dead. Dozens were mutilated: a wing blown off, a leg, half a head. They careened and stumbled in the bloody ooze, croaking and twittering, crazed in their dying, leaping for the air, the sky, broken and blind.

The sight of them was intolerable to Michael, who, covered with gore, stomped to death one after another, even seizing a few, squeezing the last flickering life to a dead pulp in his hands. He choked back his cries of loathing and despair, muttering when he could, only two words, over and over: "Good God! Good God!"

When the last bird was dead and he and Christine had crawled beyond the lake of blood and feathers, he found the pillow.

Half-crazed himself, he stared in a stupor at the grinning child's face.

"What's this?"—his wild eyes turned to hers.

Christine opened her mouth, but it was impossible to explain. How could she tell him, *now,* at this moment, about their Egyptian baby?

She shrugged and smiled, looked at the pillow with the greatest curiosity, as if she didn't know how in the world it had gotten there.

TWO

AN APPLE ORCHARD grew to the northwest. With no one to tend it over the years, it had seeded itself, the wind rolling the falling apples a bit closer to the house each year.

Finally, like Hamlet's forest, trees eventually buttressed the very walls, broke through two of the lowest windows, and then moved in. An astonishing sight! In one large room where the floor had rotted enough, the apples fell through to the dark earth below; then, wildly tropistic, root and branch, pale tendril, leaf ate into cracks of light and fissures of darkness in the decaying walls, turning, twisting, spreading: a weird osmosis that turned room into tree and tree into room.

It proved a delight to the children who, in summer, were able to crawl mysteriously through the leafy walls, and in November, climb to pick from the ceiling the green misshapen apples, so achingly sour that the merest

19

taste, the tiniest break of small teeth through cool crackling skin was enough to evoke howls of laughter and woefully agonized faces.

The "apple room" or "tree room" as it was eventually called, had been the only good reason Christine could think of to live in the house. Otherwise, to her, it was pathos-old, and sat upon its hill with the giant dead oak behind it like a tired old spider taunted by a stick.

A bright student of architecture might have been able to define its uninspired and multiple sources, but all Michael was able to tell her, and she didn't care at all, was that he was sure it was part Tudor, part Colonial, and a bit of ornate, wedding-cake Victorian, built in the twenties (said the agent, whose name was Andrew Blake), abandoned in the thirties, now owned by a corporation whose principals had to dig deep into ancient files to be reminded that it existed at all.

"Is it haunted?" Christine asked.

Perspiring, suffering a mild attack of hay fever from the cloud of pollen that hung like a haze in the golden air, Mr. Blake had to sneeze before he answered. Or perhaps he purposely delayed in order to imply something tauntingly positive. He was not naive, and a house with an authentic ghost frequently brought a much higher rental. In the end he decided not to lie.

"Well—no; no it isn't; it really isn't." He smiled his regret. "However—" since the very young and extraordinarily beautiful wife seemed so clearly disappointed "—I *do* have *another* house where, several years ago, a bit of poltergeist phenomena was reported, if you're interested in *that*." He now looked with closer interest at the husband, or was he just possibly the girl's father? Under well-cut Levi's and flowered shirt, the physique seemed that of a young athlete, but there was much more gray than not in the thick hair that was worn in the fashionable, presumably "campus" style of the moment. The face skin was clear and tanned and if there were lines, and there were quite a number, they were confined to a webbed area around the eyes and carefully softened by the gray-brown tint of his thick-rimmed glasses.

"But I'm afraid," Mr. Blake went on, "that the house is nowhere near campus. Nowhere! You'd have a good two-hour drive every day, while from here—" an easy gesture to the road a hundred yards below "—you'd have less than forty minutes. Which is respectable. Wouldn't you say?"

Michael nodded vaguely and turned to look at the house once more. A monstrosity, without doubt. But not really depressing as many houses can be. It seemed, absurdly, to have a sense of humor, laughing at itself and the eclecticism that had put it together. And if it was just a bit spooky, as Christine had observed, it had every right to be, considering its isolation, its age, its partial decay.

Thirty-two rooms!—but the whole northern wing over which the gnarled apple trees broke in a frozen wave had been so battered by winter winds and raging storms sweeping up from the valley, that it was quite unlivable, indeed, even dangerous to walk through.

The roof was gone over one entire sub-wing, and the windows, boarded and surfaced with tin, were now in ruins, the discolored metal curling in the air like burnt skin.

The southern wing, however, enjoyed relative protection from the weather and had remained in fair condition: at least ten rooms, two up, seven down, including the kitchen, were in good shape.

Michael said that five or six of the ten could be easily refurbished—with a combination playroom-nursery for the twins and a study for himself. He looked inquiringly at Christine, but she seemed in a sudden sullen mood and didn't express an interest in a room for herself. Michael couldn't believe it. "Don't imagine you'll share *mine!*" He had too many books, too many things of his own, and the room he'd decided he'd like for a study—next to the large sunny one that should probably be the bedroom—was certainly too small anyway, to hold that huge, ugly trunk (once her father's) which she insisted on taking everywhere, and the sewing machine she'd never learn to use, as well as that dusty, dried out corpse of a manikin that tagged after them like a poor relation.

He was thinking, Michael said, with a sly wink at the real estate agent, of putting the dress dummy down as a deduction on his income tax.

"We could make out she's your sister," he told Christine. "Certainly she *looks* like you. The same measurements exactly; isn't it so?"

"*You* should know," the girl replied, "you've made love to her often enough."

"That's because I thought it was *you*," Michael smiled; "—all wire and sawdust and nothing up here"—indicating his head—"whatsoever. I couldn't tell the difference."

Mr. Blake sneezed again, and having been a captive audience to the bickering, though it did seem quite a playful, even possibly loving kind of teasing, decided that they were definitely not father and daughter. No no; they were married: Mr. and Mrs.—what was it now?—*Kouris*; yes, that was it. Polish. Or Greek. No doubt it had been a May-December romance, or—with another slightly more generous look at Michael—perhaps a May-*November*.

He tried to appear entertained, to laugh a little at their banter, even join in.

"I don't think—" he told Mr. Kouris, a bit too gravely "—that the IRS *allows* a sister-in-law."

"Well then . . . my mother," Michael replied, bored with the joke.

As it turned out, Christine *did* want her own separate room, but she wanted, as usual, the best for her purpose—for "Meditation" ostensibly, for "Being Sometimes Alone," she informed Michael sweetly, and one as far away from the others as possible, and that took a bit of looking.

She decided on a small room at the very top of the house, the attic's attic really, with a round window that seemed like a porthole, the angular ceiling under a peak of the roof making it look even more like a cabin on a ship.

When the van arrived, she had all her "private things" as Michael called them—a clear euphemism for "junk"— moved in: her precious trunk, the sewing machine which (it was true) she'd never learned to use, the dress manikin that had been molded from her own body, and all her boxes of costume jewelry and make-up, together with countless cartons of "dress-up" clothes, these having more of a theatrical than a Sunday-best connotation.

The very next day she had a locksmith from the village drive up in his truck and install a heavy padlock on the door.

Michael, with no reason whatsoever to go to the attic's attic, doing so one Saturday morning only because he'd found a few loose shingles in the drive and thought the roof might have sprung a leak, didn't discover the lock until weeks later.

* * *

When he did he was surprised and puzzled. And not a little dismayed.

Why had she done it? For spite? To prove to him that what *he* considered "junk"—whatever it might be—was to her of genuine value. Could it be that? And after thinking about it carefully, he had to conclude that it was simply a matter of trust; she didn't trust him any longer. Clearly, she didn't want him looking, meddling, *prying* into her "secrets."

Not that he ever had. Or would. Not that he *could,* since the trunk itself was equipped with three locks, a center one, and latch closures at either end that also required a key.

Actually, he had seen the trunk only a few times: twice when they'd moved and it had been necessary for Christine to have it carried from its hiding place, and a third time when they'd honeymooned in Greece. The trunk *had* to come along! He'd been both astonished and annoyed at the inconvenience and remembered thinking at the time: *I've married a vampire's daughter!—she's got her father in the trunk!* Certainly it was big enough, and proportioned exactly like a coffin. But at eighteen, Christine was acutely sensitive, and remained so childlike, even childish in so many ways, that in some—in this case her obsession with the trunk, her father's only "legacy"— he chose not to tease her. So off it went to Greece with them—and back: locked, bundled, wrapped many times in a large Persian rug, intricately tied and knotted with rope.

What was really in it? Letters? Scrapbooks? Dolls she had loved as a child? Things of her father's? All that remained of her childhood, perhaps: pathetic reminders of a lost, passionate devotion to a man she'd adored.

He didn't know. He didn't care. Her design for privacy may have been elaborate and vaguely insulting to him, but, looking at the heavily padlocked door, he decided to forget it, not to mention it at all.

Besides, they weren't actually *in* the house at the time; the workmen were still there, and with so much to do and think about, Michael's accidental discovery moved into the realm of trivia.

After the wires for electricity and telephone had been strung from the road lines far below, he had to worry about the plumbing. The toilet continued to back up occasionally, and rusty water, frequently almost black, poured out of the faucets; once he had seen a tiny dead mouse choke its way through.

When these problems were solved, there were others, minor sometimes but irritating. For one thing, not only a family but a whole generation, it seemed, of giant black water beetles inhabited the house, at least made their nest somewhere nearby. Michael detested them, as well as almost all insects in general. This proved a source of delight to Christine, who, with clear impudence and enjoyment, could pick them up live and crackling in her hands. The children liked them too, and had three of them caged, like crickets, ostensibly to teach them "tricks." But Michael, with one pail of fresh plaster after another, spent whole afternoons looking for and sealing up every hole and crack he could find.

In all, the repair and refurbishing of the living area of the house proved almost double the cost of Michael's estimate, but with rent payments so low (hopefully witty Mr. Blake had said the corporation ought to pay *them* for living there) he suspected he might be able to recoup what he'd invested in less than a year.

So reassured, he was inclined toward extravagance,

dipping into funds to pay for twenty tons of white pebbles which, after a carpet of crabgrass and weeds had been removed, were dumped and raked into a long graceful drive which he made the workmen curve up and then away from their handsome freshly painted white pillared door.

"Well, what do you think?"

It was Michael who asked, so proud and pleased he required no answer, his face sunny with pleasure as he watched the last of the lovely white pebbles, as glossy as chipped polished marble, being spread carefully into place.

Christine was sullen and silent as he removed her bloody clothes and kicked them into a corner of the steamy bathroom.

Never had she seen him so angry and upset, but after he'd ranted and raved and twice seemed on the point of hitting her, he calmed down.

Much of the blood had dried on her skin and was stuck with patches of dark feathers which he picked off with meticulous care. He didn't want them floating in the bathwater, washing down the drain. God knows, they continued to have enough trouble with the pipes the way they were without clogging them up with starling feathers. The man who came with his coiled metal snake and whirring blades charged a fortune and a half each time.

Though he tried, now, to be outwardly calm, a knot of anger and exasperation remained in Michael's chest. Later he'd sip some boiling water with baking soda, or perhaps he'd be better off with a scotch or a tranquilizer. Maybe both. He had some valium somewhere. How was he to get all the work done he'd brought home for the evening? Grades were scheduled to be posted by noon the following day and his students would be milling ten deep around the bulletin board. Well, they'd have to wait. It was possible he wouldn't be at school at all, not with that unholy mess at the end of the garden. *Something* had to be done, though he doubted there was a category in the Yellow Pages called "dead bird removers."

All this time—from the moment he'd found Christine under the tree—truly monstrous, slipping and stumbling in the gore, she had concealed something in one tight fist. Knowing Christine, he knew it was something unpleasant, but sometimes if he waited long enough without any display of overt curiosity, a game would lose its appeal.

At the moment, God help him, she seemed to have three or four games going simultaneously. One was clearly the "I'm-a-Severe-Catatonic-and-Can't-Move-a-Muscle" game, so one at a time, he had to bend her knees, lift up her legs and guide her into the tub which was now almost brimming with warm sudsy water.

"Sit down, Christine,"

She wouldn't, so he had to press down on her shoulders until she gave way and was sitting. Lord! She seemed more impossible to live with every day.

The question came with the regularity of a metronome and with about as much emotion.

"Where did you get the gun?"

No reply.

Eyes half-lidded, bottom lip stuck out. Seven years old. Perhaps less. She was playing the "I'm-a-Naughty-Girl-and-Deserve-to-Be-Punished" game. Worse: there might be a "Come-On-Hit-Me-I-Enjoy-It" ploy mixed with it.

The first game of this kind had started a few months ago. They had just put Jamie to bed with a cold when Christine, the moment Michael's back was turned, im-

mersed an oral thermometer in a cup of warm soup by the
child's bed and showed it to him with the silver streak of
the mercury risen to 105 degrees. He was so stunned he
didn't think twice. With a leap he was on the phone
shouting for an ambulance, then filling an enema bag
with warm soapy water while yelling for Christine to find
the rubbing alcohol.

When he learned the truth, he hit her, really hard, chas-
ing her through the house, then belting her again halfway
across the downstairs hall. She collapsed in a mixture of
laughter and tears and he was down on his knees beside
her, babbling an apology, consumed in a passion of grief
and amazement because, whatever her distress, she was
at some level of awareness, enjoying it all.

The intern and the ambulance driver coming in at this
moment, followed by the police, thought *she* was the patient, and Michael, half speechless, considered it best not
to explain, simply stammering: "She had a fall—down
the stairs."

They were very angry; indeed, the doctor's remarks
were quite abusive because all he'd been called out to
treat was a laughing, slightly hysterical girl with a
superficially cut upper lip and, possibly, a strained muscle on the left side of the groin.

With quick rough gestures, he fastened a Bandaid
above Christine's mouth, and rose, snapping his black
bag shut.

"There's nothing *wrong* with your daughter, Mr. Kouris"—writing something in a little book. "But there *may*
be with *you*."

And with that they all left, the younger of the two po-
licemen closing the door with a slightly sheepish grin.

"How odd," Christine murmured, smoothing her long

blond hair. Her face was calm and rested. "What an unpleasant young man. He must be a very bad doctor; when he operates, I'm sure he must cut out all the wrong parts."

She looked at Michael and was surprised to find him angry again, his lips a line, his eyes blinking rapidly, half shut. It was necessary, therefore, to hug him and stroke him and tell him she was truly, *truly* sorry.

Michael bore the embrace with a puzzled frown, listening to a loving, whispered voice in his ear say in the smallest and most contrite and pathetic of tones that she'd *never* meant the "joke" to go that far. But the words he heard seemed shallow, strangely, almost eerily empty of truth, and the whole incident left him shaken and depressed.

Indeed, it was because of it that he made arrangements for her to see Dr. Ellenbogen. She began visits without the slightest protest, obviously because talking with a psychiatrist was *another* new game, one which she might just possibly enjoy.

Michael removed his own bloody clothes with a headshake of revulsion, and dropped them to the floor on top of hers.

It would be impossible to clean them; I'll throw them all into the incinerator.

"*Where* did you get it?" He was back at the gun. "Did you have it hidden? *Tell* me."

Silence.

The actual taste of blood was in his mouth, and blood was dry and tight over most of his exposed skin. Unable to wait, impatient to get it off, he stepped into the tub and sat down facing his wife.

"Don't you know what you did was a crime? Even possessing a gun is a crime, no less using it. You're a criminal, Christine. I should report you. And maybe I'll do just that."

He reached for the shampoo and began sudsing the blood from his hair. "A few days in jail teach you a lesson. You'd look good behind bars. You'd probably be comfortable, too, piled in with all the hookers and dykes."

She clearly wanted to laugh at this, but suppressed it, the muscles of her jaw drawn tight, two tendons in the neck visible.

"I'd bring the children to visit. Let them *see* their mother where she belongs."

No matter *what* he said or did, it finally became part of a game she was making him play. The name of this one was probably: "Go-on-with-the-Silly-Monologue." He'd stop it.

"Where did you get the gun, Christine? Was it in your trunk?"

Her eyes flickered the tiniest bit so he knew he had struck a nerve. And like a sadistic dentist he kept probing.

"Well! *In* your trunk, along with the hand grenades and dynamite, no doubt. Did it belong to your father? I'm surprised. I thought he was a hunter, a skilled hunter. That's what you told me, Christine. All you can do with a shotgun is *butcher* animals."

Even that didn't get a rise, but he noticed that whatever she'd been holding in her fist was now gone. He guessed it had been a starling's eye or a claw. He'd know soon enough, as soon as the water drained from the tub.

"Maybe one day soon, I'll have a look in that trunk . . . that *mysterious* trunk of yours . . . "

He had no idea of his own power or the astonishing strength of the words "look in that trunk."

The doll came to life, splashing angrily at the water, her expression one of hurt and latent challenge.

"How can you *say* things like that? Why do you begrudge me my few memories . . . all the dear, pathetic things that belonged to my father?"

"All the dear, pathetic things," he mimicked. "Like a double-barreled shotgun?"

"Michael, the gun's mine; truly. Of course he *gave* it to me and taught me how to use it. But it was necessary; there were reasons, reasons. You *know* the kind of life I lived, how dangerous. And I kept it afterward—oh, *I* don't know—because it was in the bottom of the trunk, that's all. I never thought to throw it away. All the other things he left me are private, deeply personal; if you saw them you'd be ashamed you wanted to look; they would be silly and meaningless to you, or to anyone—except me. And my father."

It was a strange, impassioned speech for Christine, and he didn't believe it; she was lying about something, because she chose to go on, growing altogether too barbed.

"Do I pry into *your* affairs? Do I try to discover, do I *care* which of your oogle-eyed students you plan to sleep with next?"

He would have counted it a blessing if she *had* cared; perhaps then there wouldn't *be* a succession of "oogle-eyed" students.

"Dear Nora—" he began. It was a reference to *A Doll's House*, and he regretted the name the moment it slipped out because the joke had worn pathetically thin. "If you were in *any* way the woman a man . . . "

"*Don't* call me Nora!" She was close to shouting. "And don't tell me that same other nonsense all over again. We settled that years ago. Besides, I've given you two beautiful children."

As if *that* were relevant.

"Given them to me! I thought they came from another planet! —Or Atlantis, or Mu—wherever the hell *you* came from! The way you've brought them up, I practically faint everytime they're friendly enough to call me *Daddy.* Christine—! They have no pupils in their eyes; they glow phosphorescent!"

Christine's cheeks reddened slightly, the jaw muscles again tightening. Obviously, she found the joke almost irresistible, but her stubbornness persisted; she still wasn't prepared to give in and sank back into the tight-lipped silence of her sulky, obstinate mood.

Michael shrugged, suddenly bored. Why must *he* be the one, so often, to make the concessions? Besides, the warmth of the bath had calmed him; he felt relaxed and oddly happy, even a bit silly. Like love to death, the antidote to the fright and drama of the starlings was surely laughter and nonsense.

So, like the crew-cut, lip-rouged movie hero in a '30's musical, he began, with appropriate gestures, absurdly to sing.

"What-ever *hap*-pened . . . to the *girl* I *mar*-ried? . . . *Where*—has all the—*sweet*-ness gonnnnneee . . . ?"

But there was no pleasing her. There the wretched child sat, soaping herself in a somewhat abstract, meditative way, stylized, divinely mannered and postured, pleasing only herself, as if she were alone in the bath, the room, the world.

Where *had* all the sweetness gone?

Not to mention the sanity—not that there had ever been very much of that! Still, that had been part of her fascination, the sweet, intolerable necessity of having her.

Christine the fair . . .

Christine the lovable . . .

Christine the lily maid . . . of Astolat . . .
How often, love-drunk, bridal-night silly, he had whispered endless lines of poetry into that whitely pink and
seashell-perfect ear that was now being washed with
such self-absorbed, scrupulous care!

> *. . . Where could be found face daintier? than her*
>   *shape*
> *From forehead down to foot, perfect—again*
> *From foot to forehead exquisitely turn'd:*
> *"Well—if I bide, lo! this wild flower for me!"*
> *And oft they met among the garden yews,*
> *And there he set himself to play upon her*
> *With sallying wit, free flashes from a height*
> *Above her, graces of the court, and songs,*
> *Sighs, and low smiles, and golden eloquence,*
> *And amorous adulation . . . 'til the maid . . .*

Ah, now. " . . . 'Til the maid—?" The next line elud-
ed him.
But how curious the mind that he should have thought
of these lines! Sir Lancelot had refused the "lily maid's"
love with "Yield your flower of life to one more fitly
yours, not thrice your age. . . ."
On the other hand, Christine was clearly not likely to
die of spurned love and float on a flower-strewn barge to
her graveyard. Indeed, he'd probably have to go mad and
kill her—*"high in her chamber up a tower to the east."*
The lily maid's "exquisitely turn'd" foot was now out
of the sudsy pink water, being scrubbed with a nail
brush, five adorable toes, some of which, at his loving be-
hest, had countless times gone to market, and some
stayed home—all having been so frequently, feverishly
kissed he could easily, at the time, have qualified as a foot

fetishist—indeed, hopeless, helpless fetishist in general: foot, thigh, breast, buttock, armpit, kneecap, throat, backbone: simply name the part. . . .

"Songs, sighs, and low smiles," he said aloud but softly, cocking his head teasingly to smile at her. "And golden eloquence . . . And amorous adulation . . . "

Where had all the sweetness gone?

He remembered Elvira—"I *adore* your wife!" —leaning the stick of her body almost thirty degrees against his at the very first of Christine's faculty "teas." "—You sly old goat! wherever did you *find* her?—and what does she see in *you?*—Quasimodo!" —her laughter shrill and giddy, at least three martinis too high in pitch.

And because Elvira was the wife of the Dean (who across the crowded, smoky room was shaking angry pink jowls at her), he managed to murmur idiotically: "Elvira— when I knew I couldn't have *you,* I simply *had* to settle for Christine."

Still, this bit of desperate flattery brought a shriek of delight from the silk-sheathed, basic-black stick, the acute angle now almost forty degrees, and in the next dreadful moment, ninety: unconscious on the floor. He hadn't even had the sense to catch her in her falling.

How sweet Christine had been! Sensible, helpful, resourceful—exactly right! Tucking Elvira into the bed in the spare room, thereafter soothing and then so absolutely enchanting the Dean that the disgusting incident of his wife's passing out at the very first of the year's faculty teas acquired the aspect of a sudden brief shower on an otherwise perfect day.

Christine *the fair* . . .

Christine *the lovable* . . .

Yes, she had been a fantastic success initially, the year's *coup de théâtre* for the teaching hierarchy.

Of course, the amount of saliva that accumulated under his colleagues' tongues could probably have been
counted a sea, but a single finger reached in the child's
direction would have been labelled pedophilia, and the
wives, while possibly aghast at her beauty, protected
themselves with effusions of doting maternity, considering her too young and absolutely extraordinary to con-
tend in any way as a serious rival.

And curiously, like Eliza Doolittle, even Christine's
occasional, shocking bad grammar, her infrequent but,
when they occurred, abysmal illiterate *faux pas* were
considered deliberate and mocking—refreshingly vulgar
bons mots to shake the cobwebs from the dusty heads of
all the musty-mouthed professors and their perfect
wives.

Christine bore the responding hilarity she evoked at
these times with such straight-faced and stylized grace
that Michael himself (though he knew better) sometimes
preferred deluding himself by wondering if the remarks
weren't deliberate after all. Even years later, after so
much living with her, he still pretended he could never
quite make up his mind.

But delight she was. And because of it, she was lion-
ized.

"But *where* is Christine?"

"Where *is* your darling wife?"

"Heavens! You're not *alone?*"

"Isn't that *divine* girl *with* you?"—lines of disappointment and dismay drawn on their faces as frank and bold
as scrawls on a nursery wall.

"Oh, pooh!" Elvira would say. "It's *only* Michael!"
And he'd be left alone at countless open doors to find his
own way to the punch bowl, the champagne buckets (if it
was Elvira's bash), and, usually, a hideous array of pastel
pink and green hors d'oeuvres: invariably vegetable-

dyed cream cheese squeezed from a cake-decorating tube onto rounds of damp white bread, each topped with an abominable twist of anchovy.

Christine enjoyed it all: cheeks flushed, eyes bright, costumed (never "dressed") in something from her "theatrical wardrobe" which, the next day, after the shock of it had worn off, campus gossip described as outrageously chic—the point being that the fantastic girl could have worn nothing but a string of pearls (God help him, the time was to arrive when, literally, if she "entertained" at home, she wanted to do exactly that) and gotten away with it.

"Michael, I must run. I'm to—"

I'm to—"present this year's Acting Awards for the Speech and Drama Department . . . "

I'm to—"introduce a real, live, living, famous author to members of the Literary Society. He's going to tell us *all* how to write a book, and why we *must!*"

For more than a year, virtually every sentence after the *I-must-run* began with an *I'm to*—until the biggest *I'm to* of them all: her pregnancy.

Rapunzel, Rapunzel, let down your hair . . .

Her "tower" at the time overlooked Riverside Park, just a few blocks southwest of the University, and if there were any more acting awards to present, and live, living authors to introduce, they had to wait while Michael spent nine of the happiest months of his life.

Christine, supine and sensuous, subtly dramatized her pregnancy, much less a mother-to-be, for which she had absolutely no talent, than a helpless, loving convalescent child—at which she excelled—demanding and enjoying every attention the doting, overindulgent Michael could provide, from daily breakfasts in bed to (since she de-

spised TV) endless late afternoon and evening hours of
his reading aloud, sometimes, 'til his voice grew faint
and hoarse, while she knitted or sewed or toyed with the
pieces of a giant jigsaw puzzle she couldn't possibly put
together.

Poems, even those she didn't understand (and these
were many) she enjoyed immensely, listening to the
"beautiful words" with frequent, contented, blissful
sighs, her body—possibly the only time ever—fully his:
rested and resting against him: perfectly surrendered, relaxed, her breathing soft and slowly rhythmic while his
gentle, well-practiced voice made lovely flowers of the
language, pausing sometimes for sweet, light kisses between bouquets of Wordsworth or Tennyson, Browning
or Keats.

She preferred epic poems, or, at least, those that in
some way "told a story." And fairy tales! These would
more than do, even the same one over and over every other week or so; and, if tired of paraphrasing momentarily
to rest his eyes, he changed or missed a word, there was
no escape: her body stiffened and it was necessary to go
back and say the word or words *properly*.

Sometimes, bored or teasing, he deliberately changed
the words; or the words in the same story but in a different book might be already changed. Either way, the
storm broke.

"No, no, no! The Beast says, 'Do you *love* me, Beauty?
Will you marry me?'* —not *'Wilt thou have me as thy husband?'* "

"*But angel*"—kissing her—"this may be the *same* story
but it's in a *different* book; the other went back to the library weeks ago! Don't you understand? The story's a
translation: La Belle et la Bête, and different transla-
tors . . . " He paused. "Actually, 'Wilt thou have me' is

probably closer to . . . " He took both her hands in his.
"You see, love—in the French language, there is a *personal* form of address, used only for one's *intimate* friends, and family, as well as servants . . . "

He stared, speechless, into grave censorial eyes, then gave her back her hands and picked up the book, reading: " 'Do you *love* me, Beauty? Will you marry me?'

" 'Oh!' cried Beauty, 'what shall I say?' for she was afraid to make the Beast angry . . . ' "

Wilde was new to her, and the first time he read *The Birthday of the Infanta,* he felt a drop of water hit his hand, and then another. They were tears, of course, and he looked down amazed.

"Oh, Michael, Michael!" she wept, trembling, and would not stop until he held her, heart to beating heart, with gentle words cracking between tears and loving laughter at her absurd and extravagant pity for the fate of the dwarf in the story.

He stroked her head, saying what his mother used to say to him: "Sweetness—Light—it's *only* a story!"

But it was necessary to abandon Wilde. If the *Infanta* broke her heart, *The Happy Prince* would have surely shattered it to fragments.

So they went back to the old and comfortable *Sleeping Beauty, Rumpelstiltskin, Snow White,* and the familiar, unsurprising others, including, of course, her beloved *Rapunzel.*

More boy than girl, it seemed, Christine's hips were slim, the pelvic structure narrow.

The doctor had several times warned her of the "possibility" of a "difficult" birth. Both words proved the grossest, most deceptive of euphemisms. When the cycles of final pain enveloped her in all their bone-crushing, marrow-piercing immensity, she prayed, clinging, nails digging into Michael's palms, to be Joan at the stake. Rather a cyclone of flame hissing around her: a final skull, scorched skeleton as sheaths of blackened, cooked flesh slid from the bone!

They finally punched her full of morphine, and the doctor's blood-splattered mask, the sweat-dripping brow that the nurse kept reaching for with folded gauze was surely God's face: she had died and was being resurrected; ah—into God's wide arms she was flung, awash in a sea of ecstasy.

Days later, when the two astonishing heads, swaddled in white, were brought in for her to see, but not to touch, she thought they must have razed an ancient Egyptian tomb to find such withered mummies, swollen and slant-eyed.

"Not a single tooth," she whispered to Michael, cupping his ear so the mummies would not hear. He was so busy brushing the wetness from his cheeks and swallowing the pools of saliva and tears that kept filling his throat (reminded that they had almost lost Christine—*lost* her!) that all he could do was nod, unable to tell the ridiculous child that *all* babies were born that way.

"How did they *really* get inside of me?" was her next odd whispered question, and over a period of time Michael grew to understand, and accept—since he had to— that although Christine had a normal cause-and-effect knowledge of birth and "understood" it in some remote, little-used area of her brain, emotionally she didn't believe it at all.

"I have known tribes," she told him, rather secretively; "native women, you understand—the Utazi in South America—who, when they wanted babies, sat in a river high up in the mountains near a waterfall and let the stream flood between their legs. That is the way it happened; it had *nothing* at all to do with men. The river water brought certain seeds that flowed inside of them."

Michael nodded, "Hm," he said agreeably.

"Virgins, too," she continued, "because some of the Utazi women loved each other—do you understand?—they would have *nothing* to do with men, but they had many babies anyway—all they needed to raise a family, because they sat in the river, too."

"Hm," Michael said, his contentment, his relief, that "it was all over" of such intensity it seemed like a dreamy happiness-drug released in his veins. "And I suppose, if they wanted a boy, your Utazi virgins, they sat in the river facing *north*, and if they wanted a girl, they sat in the river facing *south*."

A cloud fell over Christine's eyes, their violet color darkening under lashes that narrowed threateningly, while the healing, pink, tooth-marked bottom lip where she had bitten herself days ago in her agony, came out a quarter inch or so in pouting anger.

It was too soon, much too fearfully soon to tease her! Panicked—

"Angel—! Love—! My own heart—! Let your *stupid* husband have his little joke. Of *course* that is the way the—*what?*—Utazi women have their babies. I'm certain I even read about it somewhere, at least *once*—in a book."

But regardless of where babies came from, he saw the brooding, frightening, signed-in-blood vow in Christine's eyes. It was certain she'd never, ever again sit in a river high in the mountains, near a waterfall.

She changed them, bathed them, diapered them expertly, bottled them, burped them, fondled and loved them extravagantly—but only when the mood suited her, regardless of need or necessity.

They were *alive*, of course, but nevertheless two adorable dolls with no biological rhythms of their own: only Christine's whims and play-thought.

So it became imperative after the first week to hire a nurse, or a governess, as she preferred to be called, since she wore no uniform.

Miss Hart didn't sleep in, but was there twelve hours a day, and gradually, resentfully, Christine learned how to care for Jamie and Rose; but that there was a "technique" to care that had to be learned (since she was bereft of instinct) made it all less interesting and entertaining, and before the first few months were over, Christine preferred merely to sit and watch while the hatefully efficient Miss Hartless (as she called the young woman secretly) moved about like a well-oiled machine.

She called (the useless) Christine "Little Mother" —chilling the girl to the very roots of her hair, so it was small wonder that before the twins reached their first birthday, Miss Hartless disappeared.

"Well," Michael said, "—not *disappeared*"—which was Christine's word—"she doesn't *want* to come back anymore. She feels . . . "

"Just like *that*?" Christine interrupted, her eyes round and innocent.

"Yes. No explanation. Simply that she felt she wasn't *needed* any longer. Why, I hardly recognized her voice on the phone. It sounded—it was as if I had offended her in some—dreadful way.

"You didn't," Michael added cautiously, "*say* anything to her? I mean—that might—just possibly might have hurt her feelings?"

"*I!*" (What could be more unthinkable?)

"Well—! Christine—! You *do* have a way with you sometimes, you know."

"If I have a *way*," Christine replied, "and wanted to get rid of Nosey Miss Lonely Hearts, I could have done so months ago."

Which was true.

But he continued to stare at her. "Why do you call her Nosey Miss Lonely Hearts?"

Christine shrugged, her expression hovering between put-on boredom and disdain.

"Well, she *was* strange-looking, you'll admit. I mean— with a nose so *very* pointed and sharp. If she wanted to, and owned a black cape, she could have easily gone out and passed herself off as a woodpecker."

Michael's voice verged on laughter, but was also filled with reproach. "Christine! How very unkind. We all have our physical defects—at least peculiarities."

"*I* don't," Christine replied.

Which was also true.

Michael was silent, but still sensed something strange in all this.

He persisted. "And *why* Miss *Lonely* Hearts?"

Christine faced him squarely.

"Since you insist, I will tell you, Michael dear. The woman molested me."

Michael was so shocked he could barely repeat the word: "*Molested* you!"

A moue of delicate, pained impatience.

"Well—not *molested*. Such a strong word! But an *over-ture*. How is that? Is that better?"

The parrot was prepared to bark back any word she could find.

"An *overture*!"

"Good heavens! Won't *that* do? Very well—she

touched me; she placed an inquisitive hand on my breast—so." She demonstrated. "The poor soul was extremely lonely, I suppose, and simply sexually displaced. Now. That's all I intend to say about it. It's not in my disposition to *malign* the woman. Besides, it isn't as if we needed her any longer. And the children *loathed* her. I could see that. They were deathly afraid of her nose, of inadvertent—injury, you understand. I don't know why you're so surprised and upset. I'm not. I'm quite relieved."

Michael sat on his favorite chair as if he were doing so for the first time.

"She waited—a whole *year* to touch your breast?"

"Well—" Christine shrugged doubtfully, her mind racing. "Some people lack courage. I knew the desire was there, but I was skillful in avoiding her 'unnuendoes.' Is *that* a word? Her *advances*, if that won't do. Then, when she knew the jig was up—" Christine started to laugh "—and the cat was out of the bag, she was so embarrassed she packed *all* her anal thermometers and left. I suppose . . . " Christine fussed sensuously with her hair which she had just washed and dried, standing over the air conditioner to let the full icy blast of it whip undulant scrolls " . . . she was afraid I would tell *you*—which I have, and you wouldn't want someone *like that* in the house, pawing me, and probably Rose, too, all the time . . . "

She threw herself laughing into his lap, her hair a golden tent over his head, covering his face entirely.

"Do you like *cold* hair, Michael," she wanted to know.

Evidently he did; he was drunk to the bottom of his soul on the clean, cool silk of it, the weight, the tumbled glory.

They made mouth-love under it, just a little, for she

wouldn't tolerate much, her body stiffening and pulling away the moment the play seemed serious and he became at all hopeful.

"'He looked,'" Michael said, as Christnes second and final foot came out of the bath water for a scrubbing,

>"'and more amazed . . .
>Than if seven men had set upon him, saw
>The maiden . . . in the dewey light.
>He had not dreamed she was so beautiful.
>Then came on him a sort of sacred fear,
>For silent, tho' he greeted her, she stared
>Rapt upon his face as if it were a god's . . .'"

"Dear, dear Michael!" The awesome child had actually spoken, and was staring at him directly, her foul mood broken. What had pleased her? She glanced around the steamy bathroom.

"The light *is* rather dewey," she added, and leaned forward to plant a soap-bubbled kiss on his dimpled chin. "Do open a window or we shall both suffocate."

No matter how often they occurred, Michael was never quite prepared for her Jekyll-Hyde transformations, but he was happy to see Dr. Jekyll and rose, dripping, from the soap-milky whey of the tub and pushed up the water-frosted bathroom window halfway.

"How can *anyone*," Christine inquired when he sat down again and while she inspected the wrinkled, water-soaked tips of her fingers, "stare *wrapped* on someone's face? What was she *wrapped* in—the dewy light?"

Of such is the kingdom of heaven. Michael smiled at his blessed angel.

"Exactly," he replied. "That is indeed what she was wrapped in. How well you know poetry!"

"Well I know *that* one," Christine returned, "because you said it to me often enough. Or parts of it. Everyday. In Athens."

"Did I! *Did* I!" Michael wondered, barely remembering.

"You like *morbid* poetry," Christine observed archly

"Do I?"

"Particularly poems in which *women* die, and must float down the river on barges."

"It's true!" Michael confessed. "You have seen through me. I am—as glass to a mind and a violet eye as penetrating as yours."

He was teasing her so playfully and finally so much to her liking she had to give way to sudden delight, laughing, splashing him with water. He doused her back and when a rousing fight developed, making a lake of the bathroom floor, the twins appeared, curious to see what was happening.

They looked like waifs, ghetto children, in their tattered dungarees and thin little T-shirts; both were barefoot and gorgeously chocolate-mouthed, neither of them phosphorescent.

Christine spoke to them crossly.

"What have you been into? *Look* at them, Michael! Have you opened a can of chocolate syrup?"

Michael did look, and at Christine, too—who was now vacant-eyed, instantly miles away in thought and feeling, shampooing her hair as if everything were normal.

Normal!—when he was sitting in a tubful of bloody pink water, feeling again more troubled and heart-broken than ever before in his life. Why? If words could describe it at all, it was because Christine and the children, progressively, in some bewildering, inexplicable way, *were truly absent*—"gone" from him, or at least "going" in a way he seemed unable to stop.

Either his own mind, like his dead mother's once had, was beginning to crack, or *some*thing in what he'd said about Christine and the children coming from another planet, from Atlantis or Mu, hadn't been a joke at all.

It was figurative: a mysterious, heart-stopping metaphor.

THREE

IN HIS SENSITIVE, PERFECTIONISTIC WAY, Michael
was mildly dismayed to discover that Dr. Ellenbogen's
first name was Ellen. Indeed, her card which he picked
up from a silver bowl on the polished round wood of the
coffee table, identified her as E. Ellen Ellenbogen, M.D.
His tiresome mind had to try to analyze it immediately.
Why in heaven's name would the doctor's mother, with
the name of Ellenbogen, want to christen her daughter
Ellen?

And why, he wondered, were there cards on the table at
all? What were her patients to do—take a handful and
distribute them on street corners to drum up trade?

Such was his irritable frame of mind as he sat in the
waiting room, which wasn't a waiting room at all but a
plush, expensively furnished living room with a genuine
Picasso on one wall, and, behind a glass box, a Matisse
paper cutout on another.

He glanced at his watch and precisely as the sweep of the second hand touched four o'clock, a door opened and a teen-aged girl came in. She had straight light-brown hair to the waist, tied with a ribbon, giving her an old-fashioned look, rather like an illustration from a first edition of *Alice in Wonderland.*

As Michael rose, she seemed startled to see him and after begging his pardon, asked if she could help. All of which seemed vaguely insulting and careless—for a secretary, or the doctor's daughter, whoever the child was.

"I have an appointment with Dr. Ellenbogen at four. My name is Kouris, Michael Kouris. The doctor is expecting me."

A look of instant amazement crossed the girl's features, vanishing as quickly, and then, as she approached close to him, it was his turn for surprise. She was a girl at a distance only; up close her face was a virtual map, not a single deep wrinkle but an intricate maze of superfine, almost spider-web lines. Alice in Wonderland was as old as Akhnaton peeled of his ribboned shroud. It was none other than Dr. E. Ellen Ellenbogen herself, literally tripping over her apology, reaching for the back of a chair to steady herself.

"Oh! I *am* sorry! It was just—that I expected . . . "

The unspoken words were clearer than those he had heard.

She had expected, of course, a *very* much younger man.

"I mean—" she continued, "Christine never mentioned . . . We never discussed . . . "

She let it go at that, but only for the moment. The first subject, after he was seated in her comfortable study, was his age, or rather the fact that Christine—since he had been invited there to talk about his wife—was (he admitted it frankly) thirty years younger than he.

He went on to explain, surely needlessly, since the doctor was a psychoanalyst, that "some women, *many* young women prefer older men; they are more comfortable with them, they relate better. I see you have a Picasso in the outer room." The implication was clear. "And, of course, I could mention Pablo Casals. And many others."

Most people thought he was in his early forties. And God knows he *was*: measured by whatever clock nature measured true not chronological age; he hadn't been eating organic food and diligently practicing his Hatha Yoga for twenty years for nothing.

Still, a few of his flippant chickens came promptly home to roost. *Aleck in Wonderland? Boy-at-a-distance? You're as old as Akhnaton's father!* What a cruel self-punitive mind he had!

"Perhaps it comes—" (his youthful appearance, that is) "—from associating so constantly with young people." (His students.)

"I understand you met Christine that way. In one of your classes. At Columbia."

Yes.

Second seat front, third row from the windows: all wheat-toned and shining gold: his exquisite, incomparable Christine; *his* from the very beginning, the moment their eyes met.

"I had a Wednesday evening course in writing: for beginners; not the College but the School of General Studies, and the very first paper she turned in was so bad—atrocious, really—misspelled, and ungrammatical, even an occasional word—would you *believe* it!—written *backward*—that I wasn't sure I should keep her. I mean, I *knew* I shouldn't; she needed high school English, or grammar school basics, for that matter. I learned later that she'd had no schooling at all. None. She'd never lived in one place long enough. Her mother died when she was young and her early life, all she remembers, consisted entirely of travel, one country, one city after another, until the death of her father when she was just seventeen. It was he who taught her whatever he could—though it's clear he wasn't an educated man. Wealthy at one time, inherited apparently, but a . . . do-nothing, without skill or talent, a wanderer, an occasional hunter, I believe. In any event—I remember I kept Christine after class that first time, and we talked. And . . . well, that was it."

It seemed somehow obscene that they were married *four* days later, bad grammar, inverted words, misspelling and all, but they were.

"A man of my age," he explained, "and a young woman as beautiful, as desirable as Christine . . . " He paused, uncertain of what he'd intended to say. "Well, what I mean, I suppose, is that I jumped at the chance." His brief laughter was false. "What man wouldn't?— Christine! Just to see her—for a moment—her smile, her walk, her manner—is to know why I risked everything. I *had* to have her if I could. And to engage in a courtship that lasted weeks or months seemed much too dangerous. I might lose her. No. If it was to be a mistake, let me know it *after* we were married. First, let her be mine. I had to have"—he looked up at the doctor with forced truthfulness and guilt—"I had to *have* that *child.*"

And having been so quickly truthful and guilty and faintly embarrassed to have spoken so intimately to a stranger, he crossed and uncrossed his legs, ready to leave.

"Mr. Kouris—" The doctor leaned the surprising labyrinth of her intricate face closer to his. "You are *not* my patient. Your wife is. You are entirely free to speak about what you wish. Or not to speak. Or get up and leave if you so desire. Or terminate your wife's visits. Am I holding a gun to your head, and a paper for you to sign?"

She smiled, her face crinkling like Christmas-box tissue. "No papers. No guns. But I'd like you to know"—the barest trace of an accent was now for the first time apparent to Michael's acute, trained ear—"that Christine is my *only* patient. Yes. I no longer practice. I am retired. I do some work at the Harlington Orthogenic School with autistic children, and I am writing a book. That is what I do now. But out of respect for Igor . . . " She decided to formalize it: "Out of respect for our mutual friend, Dr. Marovici, who gave you my name, I agreed to see your wife, and once I had—well, you know what happened. Instead of deciding what *kind* of help she could best use and then sending her to someone else as I planned, I have been seeing her myself. She disarmed me and intrigued me from the moment we met. She is . . . a vast puzzle, I will admit. I dislike labels; still—nomenclature is sometimes useful, but I have not been able diagnostically to say of your wife that she is *this* or that she is *that*. Truthfully, I don't know where we are, or where we are going, or what progress we have made. Amazing, yes? And that is why I asked to see you today, and perhaps will ask again. Maybe several times. I think it would be most helpful if you filled me in with facts, concrete things. Your wife is so . . . imaginative, so playful—which is charming, charming of course but also disruptive—she so likes games . . . "

"Ah," Michael said.

" . . . and jokes and teasing, that I am sometimes unable to separate what is real from what is not."

Michael nodded. "Such as—? Perhaps you would like to give me an example."

"Well—" The doctor laughed. "Let us be simple-mind-ed to start: the tree room—where she spends so much time, and plays with the children."

"Oh! Goodness!" Michael said. "It's true. A room which trees have made . . . the walls are leaves and branches—with apples in the autumn to pick from the ceiling. She told you this?"

"Yes. Then I suppose the house in which you live is also much as she described, half of it in ruins the other half—"

"Yes. Exactly." And he explained in detail until she seemed satisfied.

"It sounds beautiful. And indeed very practical. But it is quite another house to hear Christine describe it. She has a way of dramatizing things. She is marvelously theatrical."

"*Is* she." With some irony.

Dr. Ellenbogen laughed. "Mr. Kouris—you don't seem to *appreciate* your wife. I understand she was enormously successful as an actress before you met."

It was a question of course, and Michael cleared his throat to prepare himself for what he wanted to be a proper and detailed reply.

"Dr. Ellenbogen—I have been married to Christine for seven years. We were married two days after her eighteenth birthday. If she was *enormously* successful as an actress before that time, then she must have been a *child* actress. Which is possible, I suppose; I simply have no way of knowing, and no desire to find out. However, I will tell you this. She *is* an actress, and a superlative one—but for an audience of one: me. Oh, and sometimes the children; she is clever, and without knowing it, we are sometimes suddenly captive, watching a performance carefully prearranged, or, even unwittingly participating, for that matter, when it pleases her, since she doles out

instant roles like a drunken casting director. I would be
very surprised if you yourself haven't already appeared
in one of Christine's plays. Or several, since she is a pro-
digious creator. And she has a wardrobe, I might tell you,
that, to say the least, is comprehensive, affording infinite
variety and rapid change.

"She is also an insomniac, let me add, and frequently
wanders about the house at night in various costumes, to
relieve, understand, the tedium and anxiety of her sleep-
lessness. Sometimes, if the rain or a thunderstorm wakes
me, and I go for a peek at the children—to see that their
windows are closed and the blankets not kicked to their
feet—I encounter her.

"I have encountered her often in the halls after midnight. Occasionally, what she wears, and her makeup, are
so bizarre that if I didn't *know* it's Christine, or couldn't
guess, I would have *no* idea who this woman is.

"Once, I found her lying on the floor in a patch of
moonlight, a dagger by her side, and the whole bosom of
her nightgown crimson. If the slight acrid odor of ketch-
up hadn't reached my nose, I would have fallen beside
her in the deadest of faints. As it was, I pretended not to
notice. After all, I have an exhausting schedule and need
my sleep, and even during those moments when I love
her dearly, it's folly to spoil her endlessly, the way her father must most assuredly have done, and play *all* her
games. Even the best and most appreciative of audiences
weary. So I stepped quietly over what I could only guess
to be the tragic if secretly smiling remains of Lady
Macbeth and went back to bed."

It was embarrassing to confess how very little he knew
of a personal nature about Christine's early life.

What he knew best, and it sounded ridiculous, was

geography! He could rattle off any number of exotic names, places she had visited or lived in and enjoyed telling about: Sind and Punjab, Orissa, Bengal, Assam, Birhar, Gujaret. *Never* anything *ordinary* like Paris, Rome, London. Oh, no. Madurai. Rahabad. Rajasthan.

"Michael, look!"—(smoothing a map)—"this is a desert, the *Dashti-i-Margo*, which means Desert of Death. And here—do you see this tiny twisting line? It's marked a river, the Org; only it's not, it is all dried up; nothing but limestone and salt and baked clay: immense cracks and jagged fissures as if an earthquake had opened its jaws to yawn; and all along, rising up from its banks is a dead city: a ruin, simply rubble, Michael, tumbled-down stones, mile after mile.

"My father and I used to wander around in the moonlight looking for ancient artifacts, or sometimes just to play. It was fun to shout, because there was an echo: not *your* voice, but a thousand eerie others, like a church choir.

"I remember—our food ran out; oh, dear!"—laughing, covering her mouth with both happy hands—"we became *beggars*, and had to live off the passing caravans— all the drivers villains, thieves, murderers.

"After two weeks one of them picked us up, but only because my father gave the *dedji*—that's the master driver—his emerald ring and a promise of money when we reached Karharut, which was the first stop.

"I think I must have been eleven at the time, and I looked like a ragged Bedouin. My father chopped my hair close to my head to make me look like a boy because he said they would rape me; *rape* me!"—this made her laugh even harder—"as if they didn't rape boys! But, you see, a girl *lasts* much longer, being made the way she is, while a boy, if a dozen men are at him, is soon only blood and mangled tissue.

"One clever thing we did was to rub some yellow clay in spots between my legs and paste on tissue-thin patches of mica to look like shiny scabs, so they would think I had one of those dreadful diseases. And my father did too—pasted on mica—around his anus, because he didn't want to be raped either. You *know* how Bedouins are: it doesn't matter whether you are male or female, or have two legs or four: they will rape *any*thing that *moves*.

"And the food!—did I tell you about that? Before the caravan picked us up? Michael, if I told you what I ate, you would ask for an immediate divorce; *immediate*. So I shan't tell you. Only that I ate myself. You will do amazing things when you are starving. Everything that didn't hurt if I bit it off my body, I did: I chewed my nails down until they bled and then licked the bloody fingers. And you know how there's always a little dead flesh around your toes, in corners—when you have a pedicure aren't you amazed how much is cut away?—well, I ate that too. I was a little beaver with my teeth. And my father, too. Busy, busy.

"Have you ever starved, Michael? Not to death, of course, else you wouldn't be here, but have you ever been so hungry that you chewed bits of leather from your shoes? Of course, you have to be half-crazed with hunger, and delirious, too, to put your shoe in your mouth. But naturally, it is only when you *are* half-crazed, and delirious, too, that your shoe tastes like anything at all.

"But no! I look at Michael and see that he was never hungry, never starved. His fat Greek mama filled him with lemon blossom honey and grape leaves stuffed with rice and mussels. He is sleek, and fat; well, not *fat*"— nudging him, sampling his ribs, kneading his knees and thighs—"but there is meat, there is fine meat on those bones . . . "

❋ ❋ ❋

Geography.

The countries, the cities, towns, jungles, islands, plains, lakes, rivers, mountains, deserts—each with clear, unmistakable names—came so rapidly, so often, that Michael became doubtful and sometimes tried to trap her in a lie.

"And *what's* the climate *like* on Fiji? I have heard that it's filthy: the damp rots your shoes overnight, and you are constantly dripping sweat."

"Oh, nonsense!" Christine laughed with surprise. "It's not that way at all. It has a rainy season, of course, when it *is* damp, but otherwise the weather's fine—rather like Hawaii. There are mosquitos, though; you must sleep under a net, but no malaria."

"But where did you *stay?*" Michael asked darkly. "I have heard there are two main islands. Did you stay on the *northern?*—I've forgotten its name."

Without hesitation: "That's Vani Levu. The southern island where we stayed is Viti Levu."

"And the city where you lived? Was it *Parkura?*" He had just now invented the name.

"*Parkura!*" She laughed, ridiculing him. "I have never *heard* that name. P-a-r-k-u-r-a?"—spelling it. And when he nodded, she laughed even more. "You must be thinking of somewhere else. The Polynesian language never puts two consonants together, each must be separated by a vowel. Anyway—we stayed at the capital."

"Which is—?"

Her eyebrows raised. "Well, Suva of course. We stayed at the Grand Hotel. I don't know why it is, but every island in the South Pacific seems to have a Grand Hotel.

"This one had a swimming pool which looked delicious from my room, but when I got there, it was as green as a jungle with algae. And crawling with giant snails.

Oh!—and the spiders, Michael: on Fiji they are as big as your hand and forever nesting under chairs in restaurants. I remember that Daddy made me shake out my chair every time, and there would always be at least one spider, sometimes two if they were mating."

"Did you learn any of the language?"

"What language? On Fiji? The population is one-third Chinese, one-third Indian, and one-third Fijian—with just a sprinkling of New Zealanders and Australians."

"I meant Fijian."

"Learn to speak it? We weren't there that long, but I learned a little; a few words. A native woman did my laundry, putting starch into everything. I remember—my blouses didn't *fold*, Michael; they cracked."

"Could you speak some for me?"

"Fijian?"

"Yes."

"Well—let me see"—frowning, straining to remember. And after a few moments: *"Meke ja tora mahaka da moyo ka lekev kura!"*

It sounded great. Michael was impressed. "And what does *that* mean?"

"Well"—she smiled shyly. "It means—"and she smiled even more shyly. "It means, 'Brother, a limb of a tree has fallen on me.'"

Michael laughed.

"That must have been useful. And your laundress taught it to you?"

Christine shook her head. 'Oh, no. No, no. I had a little book, with phonetics and all. Falling limbs must have been a very frequent occurrence, so to say it became like an idiom. Anyway, it just happened to be something very easy to learn and remember. Katatura taught me only little things, like *Bula*—that means *hello*.

"Daddy, of course, could speak Fijian very well, but then he knew *every* language; I don't think we ever entered a country, crossed a single border that he wasn't speaking all those strange words immediately. It was amazing, because I know he never went to school—not for long; he wasn't like you, with a Ph.D. in everything. Some people just have a natural gift for languages."

Her face relaxed now, energy and excitement spent, the features softening into a fixed, preoccupied smile.

"Do you know—one thing I kept wishing—I kept wishing that a limb of a tree *would* fall on me; not a big one, of course, that would hurt me, but a small one—just so I could surprise my father and say to him all those peculiar words: *'Meke ja tora mahaka da moyo ka lekev kura.'*"

"So if it *isn't* true," Michael said to Dr. Ellenbogen, "all of it, every word, then Christine's father must have had a lifetime subscription to *National Geographic.*" He added: "And *she* a photographic memory that retained every word. I never caught her in a lie; I mean, *that* kind, about where she'd been and what she's seen."

And the doctor, who by now had heard almost as many "stories" as Michael, agreed.

"I have myself been to India,"—of which Christine had had so much to say. "And I might tell you that while I was there I witnessed a firewalk."

Michael laughed. "So she told you about that—how she herself walked on fire."

"Since I am a medical doctor as well as a psychiatrist, I was particularly interested: an objective, scientific observer, you might say."

"So she told you about that," Michael repeated, enjoying it.

"What I saw involved no deception, no possibility of faking it in any way, believe me. The pit was forty feet long and perhaps ten or twelve feet wide, filled with smoldering coals, glowing red underneath but with a fine white ash on top; the heat—even six feet away—was unendurable to me; If I had forced myself any closer, I'm sure I would have seared the skin on my face. However, I tied a rag to a stick; about a foot before it reached the pit it burst into flames. And then they came: forty, fifty natives. For some reason—presumably because clothes would have caught fire, and because it was part of or necessary to the ritual—they arrived undressed and went naked across the pit: men and women of all ages, a few carrying babies in their arms. All had streaks of bright ochre color painted on their cheeks and shoulders, clay perhaps, and their genitals were smeared with blue.

"As I watched, I could think of nothing so much as pictures I'd seen of so-called *zombies*, with their eyes so far turned in their heads all you could see were round orbs of glassy white. They seemed more dead than alive, but they walked over the pit, most of them leisurely, like strollers on a summer's day. The sweat of them, dripping, sputtering and hissing as it hit the coals and made clouds of steam about their feet. A few of them ran, I noticed, and one went hopping, all of them mumbling some fantastic gibberish."

"And what did you conclude," Michael asked, absorbed, "seeing the walk for yourself?"

"Well, nothing that others before me haven't. There were no burns worth looking at—nothing I would have cared to put even a Bandaid to. Of course, every one of the walkers had very calloused feet since they go bare-foot most of the time, but that, I assure you, explained nothing. And if you have an occult turn of mind, let me assure you nothing supernátural is involved. Its etiology can probably be found in the realm of hysteria; it's a self-hypnotic or group-induced trance so profound it protects the body. If I have seen a piece of ice raise a blister and burn the skin of a hypnotized subject after he'd been told it's a burning coal, then its converse, Mr. Kouris, is as easy to believe: that burning coals can be as harmless as ice. All of which doesn't explain the *basic* mystery: that of hypnosis itself, does it?—and we have arrived, I see, where I usually promise myself not to go: at nonmenclature. We are left with our convenient and useless labels."

"But Christine!" Michael said. "A little girl, a child of ten!"

"She danced and chanted with the others," the doctor smiled; "she was painted with ochre and blue. Her hypnotic state was, I'm sure, as profound as any—perhaps more so, considering her age."

"Not *that,* not *that!*"

Michael was virtually shouting. "But *him* . . . that man: her father! How could he have allowed it at all, how could he have even contemplated it?—*seeing* his daughter, *watching* her . . . !"

"The risk," Dr. Ellenbogen interrupted, "was as great for him. They went across *together*; didn't she tell you that?—hand in hand."

That was indeed what she'd told him: *hand in hand,* and he'd chosen not to remember, or only half believed it was true. The mere idea was too horrendous; even in lesser emotional areas it angered and upset him. When you have a father who walks, hand in hand, with his daughter across a pit of fire, how in heaven's name can you ever hope to measure up as a husband?—until, perhaps, you build your own goddamn pit of fire in the back yard and walk across it yourself!.

"Mr. Kouris—?"

He looked up, startled, to see Dr. Ellenbogen smiling at him quizzically.

"You seem lost in reverie. And I did want to ask—since we are talking about firewalks and Christine's *father* . . . By the way, his name was Damenian, yes?"

Michael nodded. "Marcus Damenian."

"Well, Christine mentioned a photo. She said she thought no one would ever believe the firewalk—so beforehand she asked one of the bystanders, an English lady I believe, to take a photo."

Michael was surprised. "Of the firewalk? Of Christine and her father?"

"Yes. I asked Christine to bring it, but everytime I see her she says, 'Oh, I forgot!' or 'I looked and couldn't find it.' I suspect she doesn't want me to see it at all. I have been guessing that perhaps the nudity is just a little embarrassing to her."

"To Christine!" That was a laugh. In some areas the doctor remained blind. So it was necessary to explain that nothing could be more mistaken. Christine not only had no sense of shame, but none whatsoever of modesty. One could hardly have called her an exhibitionist since there were no sexual or ego feelings involved, but simply, like an animal, she wasn't conscious of nakedness per se, apparently enjoying the comfort and freedom nudity provided. She frequently walked about the house without clothes and, if the weather was warm and sunny, the grounds as well, here affecting a lace parasol or Michael's black umbrella—for its dramatic *contrure*, no doubt, hoping that some passerby on the road below would glance up and appreciate this bit of camp or *affranchissement de vie.*

What was more irritating, she encouraged nudity in the children; this really distressed Michael, since Rose and

Jamie were beginning to play with each other sexually—which was presumably normal and natural in our liberated society, but Michael's early years of Judeo-Christian exposure rebelled more than a little.

"She claims," he told Dr. Ellenbogen, trying to reach the source of Christine's feelings about nudity, "that it comes from having lived in so many *jungles*, playing with native children and always being quite as selflessly naked as they."

"But I didn't mean Christine," the doctor replied. "I meant she might be just a little shy about showing me a nude photo of her father."

Before Michael could offer an opinion, Dr. Ellenbogen went on.

"It's not important. I'm simply curious to see *any* photos: people, places; an album perhaps. Surely she must have *some* pictures. They might help. They would serve to enrich my own experiences and allow me to identify more with Christine. There has been very little transference, you know, and consequently not much counter-transference. Christine and I certainly *enjoy* each other; we have our little games to play—with varying success on both sides, but games do not make an analysis; indeed, they destroy it, unless one analyzes the games themselves."

"I'm sorry," Michael said. "There *are* no photos. I have seen none, and she never mentioned any to me. A few since we're married, of course: wedding pictures, informal ones, not posed—and the children at various ages, as they grew. They're six now, and . . . "

He stopped because the doctor, half-smiling, her eyes slightly narrowed, was patting his hand lightly.

"Mr. Kouris—I assure you: there *are* photos. *Many* photos. Somewhere."

*   *   *

Two vital questions remained, and Dr. Ellenbogen had
been waiting to ask these until she felt Mr. Kouris was
sufficiently relaxed and comfortable with her to discuss
them frankly and calmly. She introduced the first head-
on.

"Does your wife, to your knowledge, have any history
of drug use?"

Michael was not surprised, since he had often, at odd
moments, particularly when Christine's behavior seemed
extremely bizarre, considered the possibility himself. But
he had to confess what he himself had concluded.

"No. She is a pill-taker if there ever was one. I suppose
most insomniacs are. I do know the top shelf of our medicine cabinet is well supplied with Seconal and Nembutal. And chloral hydrate if I remember correctly, plus a
few tranquilizers, but nothing more."

"No, no." The doctor shook her head. "She wouldn't
keep *this*" (whatever *this* was) "in a medicine cabinet. If
anything is going on, it is surely *sub rosa*."

"I don't understand."

The doctor was vaguely impatient. "I am not suggesting a barbiturate, or tranquilizers, probably not anything
acquired in—well, let us say *here*, in America, but—" She
hesitated, getting to her target tangentially. "Christine
and her father were, to say the least, extraordinary. Consider the man—what little we know of him: wealthy,
widowed when his daughter was—how old?—we don't
know; eternally restless, with an obsession for travel, an
insatiable appetite for new and unusual experiences; a
very masculine man: tall, rugged, handsome, strong, but
also a man prone to the masculine protest; this I infer, in
part, from his incessant hunting, his wanton killing of
animals; in addition, and most importantly, he was a man

who worshiped, *adored* his daughter, yet—inexplicably—denied her *essential* things: schooling, culture, and, above all, Mr. Kouris, *female* love, companionship, and care. There is no history of a governess, a housekeeper, *no women at all,* it would seem, in Christine's life. Isn't that extraordinary? Isn't it? And risks!—fantastic risks, Mr. Kouris. So consider: if a man, for example, will induce his young daughter to engage in a *firewalk* with him, why should we not assume that they, *they,* I emphasize, experimented with the hallucinogens—by whatever exotic name, in whatever unknown country? And if Christine had retained a drug, secreted a quantity of it after, say, the last of her journeys and her father's death—for occasional if not addictive use—would it not explain, at least as a respectable hypothesis, the more bizarre moments of her behavior?—for example, the incident of the starlings?

"I am not suggesting a sterile pill, of course, or a tidy glassine envelope. There are roots to eat, Mr. Kouris, leaves to crush beneath the nose, pollen to dissolve under the tongue, resins to smear into the anus, honeyed liquids to drink, and pulverized bark to rub into one's genitals. Devils, my friend, smile with a thousand different faces."

Dr. Ellenbogen now gave Michael time for a few mundane "household" complaints, understanding so well that day-to-day living was the hardest living of all. So, of course, he mentioned how untidy the house was (except for his own room which he cleaned himself), and Christine's frequent neglect (depending on the wide swing of her moods) of the children. Although the grounds were safe—remote, secluded, far from any traffic—she sometimes didn't care where they wandered, what they did, how long they stayed away. Besides numerous bruises, scratches, scrapes, and cuts, they had been stung by bees, frightened by the huge swarm of starlings before Christine got to them and murdered them all, and both of them had acquired an ugly rash of poison oak and had to be taken to the doctor for injections.

Another thing, (Michael said), self-pity growing, his voice plaintive now—he had no friends, not anymore, only the clandestine kind, or the faculty, colleagues he spent time with on campus. He wouldn't, he dared not invite anyone home, not anymore, for fear that Christine would walk into the living room without clothes, and the children as well.

"I cannot, I simply cannot keep them dressed," he told Dr. Ellenbogen. "I took off my own clothes one evening to show them how ridiculous they looked, but they hardly noticed at all, beyond being, I think, happy that I'd joined the club."

He went on to mention food: the erratic, sometimes ill-cooked meals, when there *were* meals, and how *he*, not Christine, now had to bathe the twins. He managed to find the time two or three times a week, and a good thing too, because he'd discovered lice in Jamie's hair and, later, the blush of a ringworm just starting behind Rose's ear.

He felt so . . . foolish and picky complaining so. Should he go on? Well—

Another thing—Christine's absences. Frequently when he came from school, he'd find the house silent and deserted, and it might remain so for hours before she or the children put in an appearance.

Where had she been? Well, in the "apple room" with her "knitting," or locked away in her attic hideaway—listening—along with whatever other unimaginable thing she might be doing—to a recording of *L'Enfance du Christ*, which was the only, but the *only*, music she ever played. Why? Well because—had she once mentioned it?—could it have been?—a favorite of her father's? He couldn't remember. Anyway—when the recording wore out, becoming too faint or scratched for enjoyment, she invariably bought another.

And the walks! her walking!—miles of it, whatever the weather: wind, rain, snow, sun, bitter cold or intolerable heat. Not that *that* was bad, of course, but—"Oh! I don't know!—how can she make even *walking* seem strange? It's because she isn't walking. I mean—that's only part of it. What she's doing is *passing the time*: that's the impression she gives you: she's waiting, *waiting* . . . everything is, is *incidental* and unimportant besides the—the *event* she's waiting for to happen!"

Michael apologized. Language, diction was his life, his work, and here he was speaking in riddles.

"I know that doesn't make sense but it will have to do for now." And he went on to describe the last occasion when he'd decided to join Christine in a walk.

It had been something of a "nature study" with a demented child: for there were a thousand abrupt stops and exclamations of discovery and surprise as she found and had to examine carefully a variety of minutiae: a solitary ant tugging at the wing of a dead dragonfly; a "fantastic" stone with a bit of mica he couldn't see at all because he had no reading glasses with him; pale milky-green aphids busily sucking the juice from the soft tendrils of a wild rose bush.

"Now we must dig for June bugs," she instructed, knowing exactly where to find them, turning them up and over and their backs in rows to watch them die, exposed to the sun.

The talk, the things she liked to discuss were increasingly bewildering to Michael, virtually insane. But that too seemed fake, like the "walking" that was really "waiting." Another game.

Ah, but the wind and the sun through the soap-fresh scent of her hair as a wisp of it whipped at his cheek caught his heart in mid-beat, and he looked, stricken, at the parted lips, the astonishing, breathstopping shape of her perfect child's face, the clear violet eyes melting deceptively into his for a moment.

It was too much to resist. He seized her in a rush of sweet pain, aching for what he had so long ago lost, seeking to find it by bruising his mouth against hers.

Surprisingly, she endured him; he almost fainted as he felt her hands creep behind the back of his head, pressing him closer. Her mouth forced itself open under his, her teeth closing gently and grasping his bottom lip; then she bit it clean through. Agonized, he stepped back without a sound, the blood gushing down his chin.

"It required twelve stitches," Michael said; "I have a scar; I don't know if you can see it in this light," and he pointed to his chin as he pushed the bulk of his tongue down between his lower lip and teeth.

"Ah, yes," Dr. Ellenbogen said; "a faint white line."

So, it seemed, by a circuitous route, they had arrived at the final topic of the day: that although Michael slept in the same room with Christine, he had not made love to her since before the twins were born.

"Isn't it amazing," he said, "celibate for seven years!" He laughed, adding: "I think I am far more promiscuous than nature intended me to be simply because Christine has been so damaging to my self-image and esteem."

"And Christine?"

"You mean—with whom does she sleep?"

The doctor shrugged. "Perhaps I mean that. I mean anything you'd care to tell me."

"Well, I don't know, truly. Unless it's the grocery delivery boy. He's handsome and Puerto Rican and just about nineteen. Spanish blood is hot blood. I imagine she could get a really good bang out of him, if you'll forgive the vulgarity. And then there's what's-his-name?— Mr. Blake, our real estate agent, who rented us the house and is ostensibly our landlord, too; I believe he's been there a few times, either on his own or because she's called him about something or other. And, of course, and most eligibly, there's the plumber—the Roto *Rooter* man; that's a good one—eh?"

"Mr. Kouris, I'm serious."

Michael's smile faded. He nodded. "I don't think she sleeps with anyone. And I'm also convinced that she never really ever wanted to sleep with *me*. She wanted children; that was her game; two, she told me, though God knows why, since now that she's had them she seems to have as much maternal feeling as a praying mantis. Anyway—once she'd conceived—"

"Was she a virgin?"

Michael's eyes widened slightly. "No. In our age that would seem something of an anachronism at eighteen, wouldn't you say?"

"Were you disappointed?"

"Goodness, no. I probably would have been embarrassed to have found it the other way around. Maybe I was curious, perhaps just a bit surprised. She was such a complete child that I suppose I assumed sexual innocence necessarily went along with it. And in an odd, unexpected way apparently it did. But virginity? —no, that couldn't have mattered less . . . I was so grateful, so deliriously happy to have gotten her at all.

"And now . . . Well, we have made our adjustments, such as they are. No matter what I feel, I don't intend to have half my mouth bitten off again."

The doctor nodded. "I can well understand that. But you—?"

Michael lowered his eyes, the question of his sexual behavior coupled with his age always slightly embarrassing to him—at least to verbalize.

"Well, I've already mentioned my promiscuity. And what has happened to our sexual mores in recent years you must very well know. I have the pick of my students. Truly. Virtually *all* the girls. Even if it's to be only once, they're desperate to know what a professor is *like* in bed. And, believe me, quite a number of the boys, too, none of whom, I suspect, is homosexual in the old-fashioned sense of the word. They're *bisexual,* or *pansexual,* or probably, to be accurate—just plain *sexual*: they're after kicks, experiences, sensations, heightened and unusual emotions, and maybe, just maybe, an opportunity to improve their grades without opening a book."

He grinned and shrugged. "However—I fear I am obsessively philogynous, incurably *women*-oriented."

He corrected himself: *"Girl*-prone."

Even this wouldn't do: *"Child*-perverted, female gender."

And after a few moments he told the truth in a sad whisper: *"Christine*-mad."

The Chauffeur

A rap of your finger on the drum fires all sounds and starts a new harmony.

ONE

CHRISTINE SAW THE CHAUFFEUR for the first time early in June. It was possible that the children, or one of them, may have seen him sooner, since Jamie, some weeks before, had mentioned "a man in a black suit" walking near the apple orchard, but when he was questioned later, and Rose, too, they both looked up dumbly, and doubtfully shook their heads.

"I din' see n-n-nobody," Jamie stuttered, with his usual trouble.

"*Maybe* I saw him," Rose then hinted darkly, her eyes shifting mysteriously in her head. She was so obviously lying that Christine knew it would be folly to explore the "maybe." Anyway, when they were bored with each other, Rose and Jamie often invented people to play with, as lonely children frequently do, so the incident was forgotten—until that morning in June when Christine saw the chauffeur and knew she was looking at the "man in the black suit." What happened was this:

She was changing the linen on the children's beds when she discovered a few drops of blood on Jamie's pillow. It was not dried blood, but fresh, still wet and vivid in color. Instinctively, she looked at her hands, and then went to a mirror to see if without knowing or feeling it, she had scratched or cut herself enough to bleed. She could see nothing, but now her left hand smarted and when she looked into the palm, discovered an almost invisible break in the skin, a short, fine thread of scarlet at the very center. The blood was evidently her own.

Simultaneously, she heard the stones crackling in the driveway. Since she was expecting no one, she thought momentarily that it might be Michael, back at the house because he had forgotten something. But his Toyota had developed a small hole in the exhaust that made it sound like a motorboat, and what she heard was the faint, silky purr of a giant cat, a big, heavy car creeping along so slowly that the pebbles cracking under its tires could virtually be counted, one by one.

She went instantly to the window in the children's bedroom from which, because it was the front of the house, she could see at least part of the driveway.

The car was there all right, but only the tail end visible. Obviously long, sleek, black, and expensive: possibly a Mercedes or a Rolls. It had stopped, the motor still running, and as she stared at it she coincidentally had a spell of such dizziness that she actually had to sit down. Days later, when, with her penchant for curious personal language, she described the moment to Dr. Ellenbogen, she said she had become "*unfocused*—like, you know, when your eyes 'separate,' and you see two images of the same thing. That's the way I felt: as if two *me's* were pulling apart."

The sensation lasted only a moment; in the next, she was at the window in her own and Michael's bedroom. From there, she couldn't see the car at all, but she could see the chauffeur, who was evidently several yards away from it: a tall, extremely well-built man in an immaculate black uniform. The morning sun was behind him and the visor of his cap pulled slightly forward so she couldn't see his face, which was washed in shadow, but his head was tilted upward, his gaze seemingly angled to meet hers.

He stood without moving, his legs well apart, his hands—the right one gloved—on his hips: his attitude, unless she imagined it, strangely one of slight hauteur.

On the index finger of his left hand he wore an ornate gold ring. This she probably wouldn't have noticed at all except that as he shifted his weight from one to the opposite foot, she saw it sparkle brilliantly as the sun caught the curve of it like the surface of a mirror.

Whoever the man was—and who *could* he be except a stranger who had lost his way, Christine experienced an emotion that seemed incommensurate with the situation: not *déjà vu*, but, astonishingly, *être vu*. Then the feeling was gone, and she had the civilized impulse to call out to ask if he had lost his way or wanted directions, but the room from which she looked had been recently painted, sealing the windows shut.

All she could do in an effort to tell him to wait, that she'd be right down, was to wave her hand. In answer, she fully expected his own black-gloved hand to rise and respectfully touch the visor of his cap, but it did not. He gave no sign at all that he had seen her motion. Indeed, she was not certain he had seen her at all. But again she had a brief flood of uncanny *être vu* and was sure he was looking not *at* her but *for* her, his shadowed face turning slowly in various directions.

She left the window, rushing down the stairs. If she hadn't stumbled in her haste and fallen, taking some moments to recover, she might have made it in time. As it was, it took her several extra minutes to reach and open the front door. And when she had done so, the car and the chauffeur were nowhere to be seen.

Her astonishment was acute. A hand to her throat, she turned her head rapidly. It seemed almost impossible that he could have sped down the driveway and out of sight so soon, but that apparently was what had happened. And, having happened, it left Christine with a peculiar sense of loss, of deep disappointment.

From the bathroom window, Rose and Jamie were leaning out.

"Did you *see* him?" Christine asked, looking up.

"Who?" Rose wanted to know.

"Who?" echoed Jamie. And then they were both who-who-ing repeatedly, like owls, laughing and pulling viciously at each other's hair.

Michael saw so much of Dr. Ellenbogen—twice a week, Tuesdays and Fridays after his last class—that the entertaining thought crossed his mind that perhaps *he* was the patient and not Christine.

Sense of humor or reality, the doctor didn't deny it— exactly.

"There is *never* an analysis of *one,* " she said. "I don't think therapy would have improved Robinson Crusoe's situation—if you can imagine the paradox. Do you think he would have built better fires or caught more fish? So you see! One is helped in relation to *the other*. People aren't ill; relationships are. We must work on what is *between* people."

"But *am* I the patient or is it Christine?" he persisted perversely.

He had suddenly thought of his mother again and was touched with panic as he recalled the substance and quality of the months of acute mental illness that preceded her death.

Wasn't it possible that he, too, had become totally paranoiac and other-worldly in relation to Christine—as was his mother toward a select few near her: husband, son, sister, nurse—before she took the razor in hand?

Couldn't *he* be bringing Dr. Ellenbogen grievances, complaints, descriptions of events that were only *subjectively* real or wildly distorted—part of a phantasy world he himself had created? Why not?

Hearing all this, the doctor instantly startled him by agreeing, albeit a bit slyly. *Certainly* it was possible.

"Or maybe, *maybe*—" and she laughed—maybe *I* am the patient and *you* a crazy analyst. That would be good, too—eh?" . . . ("good," he learned, in the sense of being, to her, highly interesting and entertaining). "'Skilled music,'" she had now twice said to him, "'is lacking to our desire'"—meaning, in her case, that she had heard so many things so many times that she was easily bored.

"But Christine doesn't bore me," she said; "she is *my* skilled music. *Some*thing is afoot, believe me; something is *truly* afoot," and in a now-familiar gesture, she stroked the amazing length of her hair, no longer Alice but perhaps Rapunzel awaiting a visit from her prince.

"But let us go on. Who, then, is the patient? A mystery indeed, but easily solved," and her mummy's eyes crinkled. "I'd suggest that the person who pays the monthly bill is truly the patient—at least more than the others, and that seems to be Christine, who doesn't complain. Or maybe she's paying for *your* treatment—eh?" And she laughed. "Tell me—is she wealthy; I mean, did her father leave her well off?"

—An irritating, embarrassing question.

"I know he left her *some*thing," Michael replied inadequately. He felt himself tighten, always resenting the fact that Christine paid the doctor's fee, but there was no other way they could afford it at the moment, not after he had put so much into the house. And, after all, it wasn't *his* therapy; he was there only to help incidentally, to provide whatever information the doctor required; it was for Christine's health, *her* emotional improvement and stability.

"But you don't know exactly," the doctor inquired; "she never *told* you; you never *asked*. And there are no . . . bankbooks or . . . sundry deeds to properties lying carelessly about?"

"No."

Dr. Ellenbogen shook her head.

"Such an odd household! Secrets and more secrets; mystery compounds mystery."

"I have seen occasional letters arrive from a bank or two," Michael conceded; "one fairly regularly from Switzerland, but Christine never volunteered any information, and I never asked."

"But why not? It would seem a *normal* thing to do; to 'settle' accounts, so to speak. I am not suggesting that you are a man who would be interested in a dowry—such an old-fashioned idea!—but at least to inquire, to *know*— even if not to share. Christine was so young when you married, and so childlike always . . . and with her father so recently dead—I would think that when you learned that there was an estate—no matter what—you'd make sure it was protected and secure, managed, if need be, by a responsible lawyer."

"Well, I *didn't*," Michael replied irritably. "Perhaps if she had volunteered the information I would have, but *she* didn't. Besides, I didn't care. What was hers was hers. I have things of my own. I didn't want anything to do with . . . what she had."

"Why not?"

He was almost explosive.

"I just *told* you!"

"No, no, now. You *haven't* told me. You haven't even told yourself—out loud. Let us not be a child—like Christine. Come, now."

Michael took a breath. "Whatever she has, it's her *father's* . . . it *belongs* to *him*."

"—Whom you hate, to the bottom of your soul," the doctor added. She paused. "But you are wrong, of course. And foolish. Whatever Christine has belongs to Christine." And quite gently: "The man is dead, Mr. Kouris; he died a long time ago; and Christine doesn't belong to him, but to you—to the degree that any human being can 'belong' to another. But there you sit—with absolute *murder* in your heart and no place to plunge the knife or sink the bullet."

She threw up her hands, so fragile and minutely veined they looked like cracked ancient porcelain.

"I shouldn't tell you this, should I? I should let it ripen and open like a flower, but of course you've known it all along, for years, and kept pushing it out of your mind, not wishing to deal with it directly. Mr. Kouris—"

The hands came up again: "You are an intelligent man; perceptive, sensitive; subjective, given to thought. And

you had a mother, you told me—if rather euphemistically"—she didn't spare him—"who for two years was insane, and then killed herself . . .

"So you have had reason to think about death, about
killing, whether it be the self or other: both murder, of
course: one turned outward, the other turned in. And
what conclusion have you reached?—surely the truth:
that all of us, each, without exception, is capable of murder. We are *all* murderers, given the right circumstances.
We are guilty *before* the fact. It is like that line in the bi-
ble about adultery; what is it now?—'I say unto you that
whomsoever lusteth after a woman has already committed adultry in his heart.'"

Dr. Ellenbogen laughed. "Ah, but that is severe, severe. Perhaps it was meant for the saints of the world,
and not for us poor sinners. Nevertheless, I draw the
analogy, and I say unto *you*, Mr. Kouris, that you have already committed murder in your heart. Which solves
nothing. Because the problem is that you cannot murder
a corpse, or a skeleton, or a handful of dust. Yes? But
once you lusted after this man like a hunter of vampires,
a wooden stake ever ready in one hand, a hammer in the
other, believing it was *he* who kept your wife from you,
that she was more wedded to his memory than to you.
But you couldn't find this phantom, could you!—this
spectre: he was unfindable, as untouchable finally as
Christine herself."

All of which, as the doctor recounted it, with her self-
amused flair for the dramatic, seemed to give her pleasure. She stroked her hair, turning her eyes to gaze at him
frequently and, it appeared, rather fondly now.

"So you have given up the hunt," she concluded. "You
threw your stake and your hammer away, alas. Your solution— your *compensation* for your loss I might say—is

now to sleep with as many of your young students as possible, and play childish games with your wife. You remember how easy, how comfortable it is to suck your
thumb, so to speak."

She added, with dark pleasure, moving her head close
to his momentarily, smiling with her mummy's fractured
mouth: "—While Count Dracula sleeps in his trunk in
the attic."

The joke might have startled Michael somewhat more
than it did if he hadn't long ago thought of it himself.
However, the coincidence widened his eyes just a little,
and this apparently satisfied the good doctor, who
seemed to find her own sense of humor vastly entertaining.

"What we will do," she promised, "is provide you with
a new stake, and reinvest you with the energy and spirit
that the hunt requires. If need be, if it is truly important
to know what is in it, we will get to the trunk eventually,
and open it—not with a crowbar, my friend, but with
this . . ."

Michael looked. She was holding out an extremely fine
gold chain hooked to a small gold ball swinging gently at
one end.

"*This*—" she repeated, adding, "or one of her many sis-
ters or cousins," going on to explain: "a few days ago I
hypnotized Christine. She would seem to be an extremely easy subject, highly suggestible—so I thought. And, as
you can imagine, since it was *another* new game, she was
most cooperative. Which is always helpful, too.

"She went into trance almost immediately, and then I
sought—by accident really, it was merely because we had
mentioned it that day—I sought to learn what was in the
trunk.

"I expected—what?—a quick inventory, no resistance whatsoever. But Mr. Kouris—I was astonished at the ease and skill with which she avoided the question. This is hard to explain, but it wasn't as if she *weren't* in a hypnotic trance; she *was*, but that *I* was working unsuccessfully against a posthypnotic suggestion she had received previously. Do you see what I mean?

"It was most unusual. And so challenging! The simile occurred to me that I was like a witch casting a spell only to find that a prior and more powerful witch had cast a counterspell!—Or really the other way around!—I was the author of the counterspell finding the original spell infinitely more powerful than mine. You *do* see.

"In any event, I had to give up the trunk and anything related to it for the time being. What I tried next was a deeper stage of hypnosis, and then I regressed her with considerable success—to what age, I don't know exactly, but before you were married. And I will tell you this, so you may share my relief: for a few startled moments, I thought I had uncovered a *hypnotic* self: that is, a *second* personality organized around an ego, or pseudo-ego, and I am so *tired* of those! I have worked with more *second* and *third* personalities than you'd care to name!

"So I was enormously relieved to discover it was *only* Christine—a much younger and more playful one, if you can imagine *that!*—teasing and joking as usual. This was before you had met her—so we couldn't talk about *you*; and her father was already dead, so we couldn't talk about *him*—at least in the present tense.

"And then I realized that although the dialogue was most spirited, and I enjoyed it, it contained *no* information of true value. She was as guarded as ever, and resisted, absolutely, any further regression."

Dr. Ellenbogen was silent a moment, thinking. Then—

"So I would like to try something else: a drug, or several. I am very experienced in the use of drugs, particularly the newer ones. Naturally, Christine agreed when I suggested the idea, clapping her hands and demanding an immediate injection."

The doctor made a face. "—Which speaks ill for the venture already. But we'll try; with your permission, of course. That is what I wanted to ask you in particular. It would be highly interesting and helpful, I think, to speak to Christine when she was, say—twelve years old, and ten—and younger: eight, or six, or five. Mr. Kouris—" and her black eyes glittered in the crowding twilight "—if we are to *kill* this man, we had better meet him first; yes? This way, though I cannot in any way guarantee success, we may be able to see him through Christine's eyes; virtually *speak* to him. "

The doctor sighed happily, switching on the lamp at her side. "Wouldn't *that* be interesting!?"

TWO

AFTER MICHAEL KOURIS LEFT, Dr. Ellenbogen returned to her study. There was something she should do but couldn't think what it was. Perplexed, she stood center-room, absently stroking her hair.

When she forgot things, which seemed so very often lately, she felt old and tired—which, indeed, she was, though she had often mused that the inner self, the ego, the sense of "I" grew to an ideal age and then ceased to grow at all—whether by choice, design, or refusal! So, inwardly, a girl of nineteen or twenty looked out at the world through almost ancient eyes.

So much for psychic age! Body weariness was another thing, and through bones, cells, tissues, when night came on, she felt every bit her calendar age.

She had hoped to work this evening, for a few hours at least, preferably before supper, since she worked best on an empty stomach.

So thinking, she turned on the desk lamp and reached into a drawer for her heavy manuscript.

It was written in a tiny spider's scrawl on lined legal-size yellow notepaper that already exceeded one thousand and ninety-two pages, representing five years' labor. She separated out the latest and, thank God, final section of the book on which she was now at work: an analysis and commentary that compared autistic with so-called feral children.

In her reading and research on the latter, she had retained an incredulous attitude, impressed by the similarities in the described behavior of the feral child to that of some of the autistic children with whom she had worked. So much so that she was quite prepared to believe that the Wild Boy of Aveyron, for example, and the famous wolf-girls of Midnapore, were autistic: not reared by savage animals at all but abandoned in the wilderness by heartless parents, and later found by others in time to prevent starvation, absolute decline, and death.

She turned to the last page of the manuscript where she had left off writing and read:

"Reverend Singh describes how he found the two Midnapore children living with three mature wolves and two young cubs in an abandoned 'white-ant mound as high as a two-storied building.' After the grown animals were driven off, the nest had to be broken open in order to enter, and in the semi-darkness and fetid air of this vast and eerie enclosure, the Reverend claims to have found the cubs and the other 'two hideous beings . . . in one corner, all four clutching together.'

"I must confess that I find the Reverend's account highly suspect, among other things because it was the *first* time that wolves had been discovered occupying a deserted termite mound. His later account of the development and behavior of the two girls at his orphanage, however, seemed most believable, principally because I have often seen the behavior of autistic children fit his description exactly.

"In any event, let me say that the variety of animals which, according to legend, have found and adopted as their own, human children . . ."

Dr. Ellenbogen picked up her pen, then midair, let it drop from her loosened fingers, overwhelmed with weariness. She couldn't work tonight; she was empty of energy and desire. She had spent too much time with Christine, and then, of course, Michael Kouris . . .

Ah! Now she remembered what she had forgotten; the tape machine was still on; she reached to open another desk drawer, pressed a button to stop it, then, because so much tape had been wasted, rewound to a point where she and Mr. Kouris had left off.

She heard her own voice concluding: " . . . if we are to *kill* this man, we had better meet him first; yes? This way, though I cannot in any way guarantee success, we may be able to see him through Christine's eyes; virtually *speak* to him! Wouldn't *that* be interesting!?"

She now stopped the machine, then depressed the *record* button, which activated the several microphones in the room, all so sensitive and carefully arranged they picked up even the slightest whisper. As always at the end of an analytic session, she prepared herself to add a few words of summation and commentary about the material developed.

"I find . . ." she began, clearing her throat; "I find . . ." but then sat silent, recording but the sound of her light shallow breathing. For the first time in her life, she felt too tired for even the effort of a summation. In addition—and something new in her experience with patients—she realized that she was discouraged and profoundly depressed.

I find . . . After all, what *had* she found? Her performance with Mr. Kouris had been decidedly bravura, but all her observations, whatever material she had been able to collect during her sessions with Christine seemed so heterogeneous to date, composed of so many isolated and disparate elements and unrelated phenomena that she was unable to assemble even a partial pattern that expressed, at least in potentia, a comprehensive and meaningful whole. She was able to pick up various pieces of the puzzle and examine them in detail, but rarely did one piece seem to fit the next.

If she resorted to nomenclature, the symptomology, even possible diagnoses, were easy and numerous, since Christine possessed or at least exhibited to some degree everything from frigidity (and possible vaginal hyperanesthesia) to a whole string of either real or pseudo compulsive-obsessive behavior tendencies, plus ritual and fugue state, hysteria anxieties that were acted out in destructive and sadomasochistic games and potential focal-suicidal playfulness, as well as strephosymbolia, dyslexia, orthopermania, and ornithoidalphobia—the fantastic "Incident of the Starlings" (as the doctor labeled the box containing that particular tape) being a superb example of the latter.

And then, with the "appearance of the Chauffeur," was added the strong possibility of hallucinations—though whether this was of a psychic origin or drug-induced remained to be discovered.

Yet Dr. Ellenbogen had the intuitive feeling—and she was much given to the veracity and reliability of intuition—that if she were to draw a line, so to speak, under *all* of this—*all* the clinical material and fancy psychiatric jargon, and add it up—the sum total would be zero.

Something *else* was going on, something much less immediately accessible and, possibly, "sinister." That was the fascination of it. Dracula, indeed! No wonder she felt impelled to use figures of speech, the poet being much more noetic and intuitive than the scientist. She remembered that Dostoevski had written that "every man wants to kill his father" long before Freud ever dreamed it. And by how many centuries had the Oedipus legend awaited the birth of the great father of our unconscious?

Thinking all this, Dr. Ellenbogen realized that she was, after all, doing a summation without having recorded a single word. Let there at least be a summation to the summation! And she spoke aloud—

"Regardless of the lesser symptomology, the variety of which seems never to end, and, in Christine's case appears highly suspect, as if each new symptom were somehow self-induced and diversionary, employed willfully and indeed, as her husband facetiously suggests, 'to pass the time,' my methodology as outlined to Mr. Kouris seems sound and correct.

"There must have been severe traumata in Christine's early life. So in that sense, at least, she is classic, and we will attempt to regress her, since other methods to recover the material have failed.

"What I want to know is more about Clarissa Damenian—the curiously absent mother about whom we hear so little. Above all, I must hear about the ultra-mysterious Marc Damenian and his legacy to his daughter.

"In short, we must get *back* to the father, and *into* the trunk!"

THREE

SCHOOL ENDED EARLY IN JUNE, and for the first time
in years, Michael decided not to teach interim classes
over the summer.

Christine had gone from bad to worse, despite, or perhaps because of, Dr. Ellenbogen's probing.

She had started taking a drug called MDR, and was en-
gaged in sessions that involved regression. As a result,
her swings of mood were sharper and more frequent than
usual. She was sleepless almost every night, and, to com-
pensate, perhaps survive, she took two or three afternoon
"naps" a week, each lasting six to eight hours or more.
With this as a background to their daily living, Michael
felt he ought to share the care of the children more.

He was slow to admit it, but he was increasingly wor-
ried about Jamie and Rose.

Simple neglect was one thing, and they'd had much of
it growing up—even when Christine's health was far bet-

ter; but when it concerned their possible safety, it was
another matter entirely. Leaving them constantly alone
with Christine now invited a clear amount of risk. So
much so—his mind racing ahead—that he intended seri-
ously to consider hiring a full-time, live-in housekeeper
in the fall when he returned to school, providing he
could get Christine to agree, and, indeed, if he could find
any qualified person willing to stay. Somehow he had the
feeling that one day's exposure to Christine (particularly
in one of her theatrical moods and costumes) would send
any woman (in her right mind) running from the house in
screaming hysterics.

In the meantime, however, over the summer months,
he planned to keep the children clean (for a change), and
gainfully occupied instead of running wild—perhaps by
introducing them to a few instructive hobbies via a trip to
the arts-and-crafts center in the village.

The prospects were dismal, but now that they would
soon be six (and probably much too old) he wanted to
"structure" their lives with a few decent, normal children's habits: like daily bathing, eating on time, getting
to bed before their usual postmidnight hours.

Above all, he wanted to talk, really *talk* to them—about
whatever one talks to children about, and listen to what
they had to say. They seemed never to want or need to
verbalize. Everything was monosyllabic, or less—a quick
movement of the head yes or no. Michael had watched
them when they were unaware of it and had discovered
that they seldom talked even to each other. Or they had a
private language that was more sign than otherwise. Perhaps being twins made a difference. Were they intuitive,
sharing what was in each other's head? Whatever the reason, they remained (and he was forever blaming Christine) remote and strange, furtive and secret. He had no

sense at all of their *belonging* to him, or he to them. It was this he meant to explore.

And when he found time for himself, there was an essay waiting to be finished, and a double stack of important must-read books in his study that over the winter months had grown to four feet high.

So *that*, in general, plus his talks with Dr. Ellenbogen, was to be the "shape" of his summer. And to celebrate the first day of "vacation time" Michael declared a holiday for a family "reunion."

Everyone gathered in the summerhouse with watercress sandwiches, which the children wouldn't eat, and toasted marshmallows (over charcoal in the hibachi) with which they stuffed themselves with such bad greedy aim that their mouths and Jamie's nose were white with the sticky stuff. Then Rose stupidly put a charred one to her mouth that she didn't know was still blazing underneath, burning her bottom lip. She went off screaming, leaping in pain like a wounded doe, to disappear into the orchard with Jamie behind her.

Trouble started immediately, Christine calmly knitting her whatever-it-was, without the slightest show of concern or sympathy. It was as if she had listened to the shriek of an automobile tire rather than her daughter in agony.

Michael had the impression that if Jamie or Rose accidentally chopped off a finger with an axe, Christine would murmur: "Oh, dear; now look what you've done; you've gotten blood all over my lovely dress!" So he sat momentarily silent and upset, brooding, his head lowered like a bull getting ready to charge, wondering if he was going to be able to "shape" even *one* day of his carefully planned summer. Then he rose suddenly, bellowing: "Rose! Rose!"

"Oh, do leave her be," Christine said; "it was a little hurt, and she deserved it—putting a burning marshmallow into her mouth. How stupid can you be?"

And suddenly Rose was back, a small blister on her lip, but laughing, running, climbing the lattice wall of the summerhouse, having forgotten the hurt already.

"So there you are!" Christine chided, looking at Michael severely. "You think I am heartless and unfeeling, but it's just that I *know* children and you don't. They dramatize *everything*. If you gave them all the attention they demand, they would exhaust you in a single day." And she returned to her knitting.

Michael, of course, had to agree—this time. He sighed his defeat and went back to his watercress sandwich, watching Christine's small hands, like two white birds, flying in and out of an expanse of blue and green wool. He had no idea what she was making or attempting to make, but it seemed the same old scrounged-up twisted yard or so of amorphous something-or-other that she dragged out to work on every few days. It wasn't a sweater or a scarf. The closest he could guess, being much too afraid to ask, was that it might just possibly be some sort of hideous afghan or poncho. He prayed God it wasn't for him and that he wouldn't have to open a package some fine birthday or Christmas morning and find this grimy if loving expression of her considerable labor.

He wasn't aware of how often and heavily he sighed, but she was.

"Why do you sigh?"—looking at him crossly.

"Oh—?" He shrugged. "I'm sorry. I wasn't aware. It means nothing."

"It must." Was she actually *counting* stitches! "Everything means *some*thing. My father once told me that even

the craziest things that people do in insane asylums have
meaning, that their behavior is, hm, symbolic."

"Your father."

"Yes."

She stopped knitting to look at him, her eyes in the afternoon light astonishingly violet and clear. "You don't
like me to speak of him. It makes you uncomfortable—as
usual."

"Good heavens!" She *was* surprising. "I never said
that. Or felt it. Never."

"Then why do you make faces—always when I . . . "

"Faces! What faces?"

" . . . mention his name?"

"I don't make faces." Did he? "Well, if I do, it's because you have a way of talking about your father, giving
the tiniest bit of information and then shutting up—as if
it had been a mistake, or as if you had a few horrendous
secrets to hide." She didn't reply. "Do you?"

"Do I what?"

"Have a few horrendous secrets."

"I don't know what the word means."

"*Oh* Christine! —Horrendous: big, terrible, terrifying,
awful."

She laughed. "Is that what you believe?"

His exasperation grew. "Christine— *Sweet* child—
Darling, *lilac*-eyed angel— Mother of my two *perfect*
children— I am describing the *way*, the *manner* in which
you behave. I'm not saying it's true."

"But I do have secrets."

"Horrendous?"

"Naturally. Of course. What is the point of having
small, un-horrendous secrets. If you're going to have
them at all, they might as well be . . . big, terrible, terri-

fying, *awful.*" She glanced at him with a sly, sidelong look. "I have noticed that you have a few horrendous secrets of your own."

It seemed an allusion, a reference to his sexual relations with his students.

"Oh, come, now—"

She guessed what was in his mind. "Oh, I don't mean *that!* How tiresome! I mean— Well, for one thing, you never told me how your mother died."

He was shocked. "But I did. You know very well she killed herself."

"Yes yes, but never *how,* never that. Or *why.* You've kept *that* a secret. Do you see—?"

"Oh, Christine! Not intentionally. I mean— It seemed morbid, or perhaps too painful, to talk about. And the details were—so bizarre."

She waited, clearly wanting to know after all these years, so he went on. "My mother—was depressed, deeply despondent after my brother's death. She felt responsible. I don't believe I ever told you how little Charles died. I was about six at the time; he was, well, a baby. What happened . . ." He paused. It was enormously difficult. "We had a cat, a big old tabby; been in the family for years. One day, the animal climbed into my brother's crib and went to sleep—his body apparently covering my brother's face and mouth. Charles was smothered to death."

"The cat *killed* him?"

"Yes."

"A *cat* killed your brother?!"

He could have killed *her* at the moment for her display of surprise.

"*Yes!*"

"But— What then? I was asking about your *mother.*"

"And I'm telling you! My brother's death affected her profoundly. She felt *guilty*, to *blame*—as if *she* were responsible."

"Well, she *was*," Christine said. "She let the cat on the bed. Or *you* did, perhaps. Maybe you were jealous and wanted Charles dead."

He let that bit of idiocy go, chalking it up to too many analytic hours with Dr. Ellenbogen.

"She was never very stable emotionally, and my brother's death was just too much for her. She moved into her own world."

"And killed herself."

"Yes. Two years later."

"What happened to the cat?"

Michael was silent a long time. Then he said, letting it all go— "The cat died the day my brother died. Our apartment was on the fifth floor, and when my mother discovered what had happened, she grabbed the cat and threw it out the window."

Christine's laughter exploded before quick fingers covered her mouth.

"Oh, I'm *sorry! Dear* Michael, forgive me. But even the most tragic things in life sometimes have their funny side. Imagine! Throwing an innocent cat out a window, as if it were *his* fault! The cat was really being loving to your brother, isn't it true?—cuddling up to him; I'll bet it was purring when your brother died."

Michael sighed.

"There!" Christine said. "Do you see? Sighing and more sighing. I shall have to call you The Man Who Sighs."

No comment. Michael waited; then, presently: "Well?"

"Well, what?"

"I thought we were trading horrendous secrets."

Christine shook her head. "Oh, but yours wasn't very horrendous. Besides, it didn't happen to *you*. It happened to the cat. And to your mother."

"You're trying to cheat," he complained. "Come, now. And I don't want to hear about the flora and fauna of Sind or Bagalore. Whenever we talk about you or your father, all I get is geography. Did you *really* go to all those places you name?"

"Oh, yes; that's all we did: travel and more travel. Never *cold* countries; he didn't like the cold, but warm places. I have seen a thousand propeller fans spinning slowly on a thousand crumbling ceilings."

And the very next thing she said was: "The man is coming to install the air-conditioners tomorrow; two, one in the living room, the other in the bedroom; isn't that what you said? Will you be here to show him which windows—or be sure to tell me?"

She was infuriating. And he had to remind her, as he had a hundred times before, of the peculiar *way*, the strange *manner* of her thinking, adding, resigned: "But it is the way *women* think; I have noticed it about *all* women; I see it in my classes. They think via association, and ruminate—like a cow. They simply never keep to a straight line of thought. If they do, they are thinking like men; probably they are lesbians."

"I was a lesbian once," Christine said darkly.

Michael had to laugh, though he had no reason at all to doubt her. She seemed capable of all and everything—except loving him the way he wished to be loved. And loving the children the way they needed to be loved. The thought, as usual, was depressing.

If we are to kill *this man, we had better meet him first, yes . . . ?*

"Do tell me about it," Michael invited, soberly; apparently "being a lesbian" wasn't one of her horrendous secrets.

"But if I do," she replied, eliciting a promise, "you must tell me about the time *you* were one, too."

"I don't think I was ever a lesbian," Michael replied.

"Well—"

Christine shrugged. "It doesn't matter. You were *some-*thing. Everybody is something at some time or other. Isn't it true? Tell me about all the forbidden loves in your life. If you had any. They are always the *most* exciting."

FOUR

DURING THE THIRD WEEK IN JUNE, when the New England weather usually remained cool, even crisp at night, there was a sudden foretaste of summer. The temperature for two days crept into the middle and upper eighties.

Michael, who had been born in the South, New Orleans, to be exact, and spent the early years of his life there before his mother's suicide and he and his father and sister moved to New York, had a kind of bred-in-the-bone enjoyment of heat. And Christine, too, who (if it was to be believed) had spent most of her childhood years in "steaming jungles" in various unlikely parts of the sub-civilized world while her restive father pursued the will-o-the-wisps of his unimaginable activities, also found the unexpected weather fun.

But she was inclined as usual to walk about nude, her nakedness being to her as unthinking and unself-con-

scious as an animal's. Since it disturbed Michael, however, particularly if she encouraged, as she did by example, the children to do the same, she was persuaded to
wear *some*thing. The "something" turned out to be a
filmy, floating wrap-around "aura" of transparent material that could have vied with a cloud of mist in its capacity
to conceal. It came, of course, from her "theatrical" wardrobe. He had seen her wear it once before—when she was
Ophelia, not *going to,* but *returning* from the river, quite
alive and on her own two feet—with an impressive
monologue concerning her death, obviously not Shakes-
peare's but quite inventively her own.

Michael opened his mouth to protest her unhappy
choice of attire, but a history of ultimate exhaustion and
futility in such matters soon closed it.

Besides, he was more concerned at the moment with
the air-conditioner in the bedroom, which they'd not had
occasion to use before. Now that they needed it, it refused to work.

"Are you sure it's plugged in?" Christine asked.

Because of her Ophelia outfit, another example of her
unending willfulness, Michael was irritable.

"Well, of course it's plugged in! What am I—stupid?!"

"Sometimes you are," Christine smiled, with a genuine
sweetness. "That is one of the things I like about you."
She added, poking his ribs: "Every week you start the
crossword puzzle in the Sunday *Times* and do only about
a third. I find them all over the house; and to do even *that*
much you chew the ends off half a dozen pencils."

That from Christine!—practically illiterate herself: if
she had to write him a note, it was shakily printed in capital stick letters—straight out of kindergarten, with sometimes an S drawn backward.

The window containing the air-cooling unit was

sealed, but Michael pried open the south window and tied back the curtains, hoping for some circulation of air. He then pulled the blankets from the beds, leaving only covering sheets.

An hour later, after the children were asleep and Michael's sundry nightly rituals were attended to: such as locking all the doors, making sure the pilot lights in the stove and clothes-drying unit were burning, he poured a glass of water from the thermos on the night table between the twin beds and reached into the drawer for a valium. He seldom took them, but the airless room was disturbing and one might relax him and help get him to sleep.

"Do you want one?" he asked Christine, who was already lying on her bed. She shook her head.

"Sure?"

She nodded.

"What's going to happen?" he asked; she usually knew beforehand. "Are you going to be able to sleep?"

"I think so," she replied. "I had no sleep at all last night, and only a little the night before. The need accumulates."

"What did you do last night?"

The tone was conversational; he was curious to know; sometimes her nocturnal activities were interesting.

"Oh—I read in the Tree Room for hours—with three candles. It was spooky. And there were strange noises—squirrels, maybe. The room is alive, you know; it has eyes in the walls." She paused. "And then—I guess it was almost dawn—I went to the attic and listened to music for a while . . . " Another pause, and Michael added mentally, speaking for her ". . . and after that I went through the trunk—looking, touching things fondly, lovingly; remembering . . . remembering . . . "

"And then," Christine went on, "I walked all over the grounds—with nothing on, all through the apple orchard, and down through the scrub pine to the little hill over-looking the main road. I watched the milkman come by; it was just light enough."

"Did he see you?"

"Well, of course! He always sees me, if I'm there. He looks for me. I wave—and he waves back."

"He sees you—naked?"

"*Cer*-tainly!"—surprised. "That's the point, isn't it? I'm sure he must have made up some name for me by now." She laughed. "—Such as, *that Crazy Lady at the Kouris house*; or maybe, when he gets back from his rounds, he tells all the other milkmen: "I saw *that nude nut of a professor's wife* again!"—and she laughed even more.

Michael, undressed now, and deciding because of the heat to sleep nude himself, sat on his bed and for a few quiet moments looked over at Christine: head to toe, breast to knee, navel to crotch: still his incredible, breath-taking, lovely child. If he couldn't touch her—it was too dangerous to risk—just to look at her was almost enough.

"One of these days," he said, "the milkman will get out of his truck, race after you through the scrub pine, hunt you down like an animal, and rape you."

Christine half-smiled, having already begun to drift into one of her remote fugue states that sometimes preceded sleep.

"Wouldn't *that* be lovely!" she murmured.

And after a few moments: "Oh—but I don't think he'll do that. It would ruin everything. I'd no longer be his misty, ghostly lady of the dawn, waving naked from her hilltop. After all, how many other milkmen have that?"

"Have what?" Michael asked, wanting to hear it again.

"A misty, ghostly lady, waving naked in the dawn."

"None," Michael replied firmly, "—ab-so-lute-ly none."

And that was the end of the evening's dialogue; brief this time; sometimes it could go on for half an hour or more. But Christine had slipped deeper into her fugue state, and now, though her eyes were a crack open, he knew she was virtually comatose, so relaxed she looked like a jointless doll thrown to the bed by a careless child.

Michael stared at the doll for a while, his head shaking slightly in marveled disbelief, removed his eyeglasses, turned off the lamp, and fell back on his pillow with the world's weight of a sigh.

There must have been a full moon, or one close to it, for, though he could not see it from his bed through either window, the room had a faint silvery glow, most everything in it, at least in its shadowy proportions, clearly visible.

Across the room, in Christine's wide expanse of vanity mirror, he could see her full length upon the bed. She had straightened out, no longer doll-like, but now somewhat stylized and rigid in posture, a bit elegant, her hands folded crisscross on her chest. Her gauzy outfit had been bunched carelessly above her head, a corner of it fallen across her eyes like a shroud.

"Ah," Michael thought, "Ophelia is finally dead."

It was about four a.m. when Michael woke. He lay utterly still, puzzled, bewildered with fright, thinking an unfamiliar sound had broken his sleep, but when he heard nothing he relaxed. Occasionally, Jamie or Rose had a bad dream, and it was necessary to go to their bedroom and sit for a while, or sing, or hug and rock. But the children were quiet.

He turned on his side, and doing so, happened to glance into the vanity mirror across the room. The room itself was slightly darker now, the moon evidently having lowered in the sky, but he could still see Christine on the bed, and she seemed oddly covered or half-dressed. It wasn't her Ophelia outfit, which was still bunched above her head, but something heavier and not transparent: curiously, a dark, almost black ankle-length skirt or dress, though her shoulders and breasts were bare.

Perhaps she'd been sleepless after all and during the night gotten up to wander about the house in another of her theatrical outfits, returning to the bed with it on, but as Michael continued to look, puzzled, half-stupid with sleep, one of the folds in the long skirt or dress billowed slightly, moving gracefully, as if a faint breeze had caught it. Then another fold moved, while her feet, which were bare, remained perfectly still.

All this was so singular, and odd, that Michael, still drugged from the valium and a mixture of heat and sleep, put on his glasses and sat up, swinging his feet over the side of his bed nearest Christine. He then leaned closer to see what she wore.

He had not seen it before. Was it lace? It was intricate, elaborately patterned, yet so melting into its own shadows that the material seemed to combine the sheerness of silk with the richness of velvet, so singularly light that his very movement in rising caused a disturbance in the air that made the material gently waft and scroll about Christine. And now it seemed to "grow," moving itself upward, covering one of her breasts!

Astonished, compelled, Michael reached across the bed to touch the dress approximately at the level of Christine's thigh.

His hand touched nothing, but sank through what in the first few moments felt like a vibration of fur, and in the next, an enveloping flutter of countless velvet flower petals.

When, chilled, he jerked his hand back, the dress instantly disappeared from Christine's body in a whispering whoosh of sound as the thousands of black moths that composed it and had covered her rose in an agitated cloud into the room.

With part groan, part bellow, Michael clicked on the bedlamp which, because the insects were so numerous and dense, barely lighted the room.

Arms flailing, still yelling, he leaped to the wall switch and turned on the ceiling light, then ripping a sheet from his bed, beat insanely at the air, striding and spinning wildly about the room.

The moths poured out of the window into the night like a black river. Not a single one was left when Christine, half-waking from the commotion, turned her sleep-drugged or drug-drugged eyes and saw her distraught and apparently half-demented husband across the room, standing naked and covered with sweat, a rumpled sheet in his hands, staring at her with the widest, most glittering eyes she had ever seen.

"What is it?" she asked irritably. "What's the matter with you, Michael? Go back to bed. And turn off those dreadful lights."

He was choked with unsaid words. "Don't you *know* what happened? Couldn't you *see?* You were covered with insects. Moths! Black moths!"

Something like relief and slight pleasure changed her dull expression to a half-smile.

"Oh, *those!*" she said, remembering. "Yes, I did see them. I watched them for a while, when they first came in. Weren't they *strange?*! I didn't know *what* they were doing; could you tell? At first, I was going to shoo them out, but they were so cool and curious I just let them do what they wanted."

And she was asleep.

Presently Michael shut the window, shaking, his fingernails rattling against the glass. He looked around carefully to make sure there wasn't an insect left, then went back to his bed, lights still on, his eyes for the rest of the night open and staring at the ceiling.

He could, almost Zenlike, or perhaps it was his years of Hatha and Karma Yoga, empty his mind of thought—stop the thinking process. He did so now. It seemed necessary. To think at all, to attempt a rational explanation or analysis of what he had seen, and Christine's reaction to it, would perhaps, too soon, take him the way his mother had gone.

So he rested, his "brain" virtually empty until dawn. His body, however, had its own uncontrolled and uncontrollable life: in the oppressive heat of the airless room, it glistened and ran with sweat, soaking the sheet beneath him.

FIVE

CHRISTINE BROODED OVER WHAT DR. ELLENBOGEN called "the incident of the chauffeur" (as the tape containing Christine's account of it was also labeled).

It made her angry, certainly irritated, that the doctor—though not in so many words—considered it a "hallucination"—euphemistically referred to as *"an appearance* or *the* appearance."

But the woman, after all, wasn't very bright. Christine had thought so at the time of their early sessions; indeed, the psychiatrist had seemed very much a challenge, an "adversary" worth playing, but all the games they played so far, Christine had won.

Still, she wanted the additional triumph of proving the chauffeur "real"—flesh and blood, and herself as bloody sane as the doctor herself (though how sane *that* was, was a moot question)—certainly not projecting uniformed phantoms from her head into the world; so she found herself looking for him, wishing for his return.

He was *not* a hallucination; this much she knew, and if he were a ghost or anything other than the so-called "real" of the sensate, phenomenal world, then she wanted him back even more—bringing with him, she hoped, an additional "assertion" of his *being* and *purpose.*

She remembered the realty agent, Mr. whatever-his-name, Burke or Blake, averring that the house wasn't haunted, and this contributed to her discouragement; still, every noise in the driveway or orchard brought her quickly to a window or a door, her breath short—and her disappointment very real if it turned out to be a delivery boy, or the postman on his motor bike, or, as was usually the case, only the children playing.

But, of course, as the seed contains the flower, and the thought we are going to think tomorrow exists in potentia today, Christine eventually got her wish. And she had not too long to wait.

On the afternoon of June 22nd, which happened also to be the twins' birthday, the chauffeur appeared for the second time.

Actually, Christine had not been much preoccupied with the thought of him for several days; on this particular afternoon even less so, for she was concerned with the details of a small celebration for the children.

Of course, they would *really* celebrate when Michael got home. He was bringing a large preordered pink and white birthday cake decorated with the children's names, and a few small gifts. But as a prelude, and also because the day had been so boring and she was suffering from what she called one of her "peculiar feelings"—slight vertigo, rapid heartbeat, a sense of impending "disaster,"

and itchy palms—("floating anxiety" Dr. Ellenbogen had
dubbed it), Christine had frosted three plain cupcakes to
make them look festive and centered a candy rosebud
with a candle in each; these on a tray with a teapot of
milk and demitasse cups she brought to the Tree Room—
which was now glorious with leaves and the end-days of
flowering: the floor a thick tossed carpet of bruised scent-
ed petals.

When she got there, Jamie had climbed and gotten
himself stuck on a branch in one of the walls, and, as she
was lifting him down, an open pin that replaced a missing button to hold up his pants pierced Christine's palm.
As she watched a drop of bright blood well from the
small wound, she heard the crunch of pebbles in the
driveway, and so absolutely knew, *knew* who it was, that
for some moments she didn't move to look: wanting to
enjoy, instead, like a blind person, a purity of sound un-
clouded by vision.

Again: the luxurious purr of the machine: a murmur of
oil and silk, the stones splattered and crushed beneath
the enormous weight of it as it moved with undersea
slowness.

A few of the pebbles must have gotten caught in the
tread of the tires: she could hear the metallic rattle of
them under the fenders. Presently the car stopped, and
she heard the solid click as a door swung open and shut.
Then: *his* footsteps: measured, slow, as he moved,
paused, moved again. In a moment, another door opened;
she did not hear it shut.

Silence.

Breathless, Christine turned to see if the children had
heard, but they were all eyes and hands, attending to
their birthday "tea" party, Rose pouring milk into the little cups, Jamie—who wouldn't have dared to touch the

matches if his father were there—boldly doing so now to light the candles, knowing he didn't risk a slap or a scolding from his mother.

Christine looked at their busy faces, and, agonized to know, whispered: "Did you *hear* something?"

"What," bellowed Rose, without looking up.

"Hush! Did you *hear* anything?"

"Outside? You mean—that *car?*"

Christine almost fainted from pleasure—*(hallucination, indeed)*—and moved quickly to a green leafy wall, reaching with both hands to make a small round space through which she could look.

He was quite like before: tall, broad-shouldered, impeccably uniformed in gold-buttoned black, the cap very straight and proper, the plain black boots gleaming with polish—all of him radiating an aura of maleness so potent Christine lifted her nose, virtually able to smell it. The only difference seemed to be the curved, head-fitting, thinly gold-rimmed dark glasses he wore this time.

The girl's eyes darted quickly about, fearful to turn away even for a moment lest he again disappear. She could see all of the car this time: a black Rolls, the chrome touched with a hint of yellow that made it seem gold. There was a crest on one door, intricate and multicolored, but the car was at an angle and too far away for her quite to make out.

Her eyes went back to the chauffeur. Several dark butterflies fluttered about his head, or were they the black moths!—from the incredible army of them that Michael swore was breeding somewhere in the wilderness of the orchard? One or the other, the chauffeur's gloved hand halved the air in front of his face to scatter a growing cluster that seemed intent on settling on the visor of his cap.

They circled his head and then disappeared, except for one, which he plucked from the air. Fragments of crushed wings fell from his fingertips like a handful of black confetti.

He was standing all this while by the open rear door of the car, one hand remaining on the handle, as if he were holding it open for someone to step out.

Christine narrowed her eyes, peering into the shadowed interior, but it was quite empty.

Conversion is an unconscious incubation (of knowledge forgotten or slowly acquired and synthesized) that enters consciousness with something like a burst.

So with Christine: not conversion exactly, but what she had previously understood to be *être vu:* a flooding up of subliminal knowledge whose sum is more than its parts. It entered her awareness with a small explosion or implosion of growing-if-still-partial insight that left her chilled from spinal column to surface skin, as she reversed the commonplace dictum: "he's not there because I see him, I see him because he's there!"—and he was not there to *bring* someone—the car was empty!—but to fetch someone, to pick someone up!

He turned his head this way and that, again fanning away a few of the persistent black moths, looking, searching, and for several seconds appeared to look at her directly, her own eyes to him, if he could have seen them, like a startled doe's shining among glossy leaves; but it was obvious she did not exist for him, not yet. *It was still too soon; the time was not right.*

And, knowing this much, Christine seized the wall of trees as if she'd been crucified to its branches, twisting her body, half-aswoon in the panic and pleasure of anticipation, under the wide, fearful eyes of the children blinking over the flames of their birthday candles.

Memory and Desire

He has known thee and loved thee well; take heed then; hail him, and under tides (of love) and deserts (of memory) follow him: his breath, his body, his desire.

ONE

DESPITE DR. ELLENBOGEN'S PROFESSED DISLIKE and mistrust of nomenclature, she had any number of words, categories, definitions that had proved useful in her work, but her brain ticked them off so rapidly now that she suspected that far from dispensing with it, she had merely refined the process of "naming things" to the point where, while still operative, it was virtually subliminal—thus defeating her conviction that conventional prognosis was a deterrent to important insights and intuitions, obscuring those psychic "areas" where the real work was to be done.

Christine Kouris was a case in point.

If "neurosis" (according to the doctor's own definition) consisted of, one, an impaired capacity for loving, plus, two, surrender to irrational authority, plus, three, an inability to live in (i.e., experience and enjoy) the "pres-

117

ent," then the girl could certainly claim honors on all three counts.

Her constant role playing, her display of theatrical moods and costumes, her countless "games," exhibited a clear dissatisfaction with her immediate daily life and living, although no true "inability" seemed involved— curiously, a deliberate conscious choice.

On the other hand, her "surrender to irrational authority" was more than clear, revealed in all kinds of ritualistic behavior, from the constant repetition of *L'Enfance du Christ* to her preoccupation with the contents, whatever they were, of her mysterious trunk.

And her "impaired capacity to love" was most pronounced of all, and well-documented by the countless examples provided by her husband.

Yet under this triad of neurotic symptoms that in Christine's case appeared almost classic continued to lurk the suspicion in Dr. Ellenbogen's bones: something *vital* is missing—something *else*, something *more*, something *other*.

Still, since it was necessary to start serious work somewhere, the hysterical symptoms were perhaps the simplest to deal with, their etiology, with luck, easily exposed. Not that it was important to start in any particular area, since work would be done simultaneously in all areas.

When she was young in her career, she was fond of saying "all roads lead to Rome," later, in an effort to be slightly more contemporary, she changed it to "*any* start, any *where*, is the yellow brick road that leads (inevitably) to the Emerald City (of Oz)"—both Rome and the Emerald City being, of course, the center and source of the neurosis.

Of course, this applied to the solution of the neurosis

through the recovery of repressed material via free association and the formation/dissolution of transference which the doctor, changing with the times, had abandoned years ago in favor of psychopharmacology. "Drug therapy" was much simpler, and sometimes moved very rapidly.

The immediate goal was to get Christine to *feel* again, to respond to her husband and children with genuine emotion. If this were achieved, even by degrees, the girl's ability to "live in the present" would be enhanced; there would no longer be so much absorption in the past, and less longing for whatever it was she phantasied to be her future—that now nameless *person, thing,* or *event* she desired so passionately and for which, as her husband described it, she was "*waiting* so impatiently."

Dr. Ellenbogen had given up the use of LSD and mescaline; both, she had found, produced too much disorientation; perceptions became so distorted that they added to rather than diminished the "experiential density" of the therapy process.

After much experimentation, her final and brilliant new method was soon called "ES" or "screen therapy" (E for Ellenbogen and S for screen) because the patient's experience was similar to that of attending a motion picture. It involved the combined use of harmaline and ibogaine. The drugs, both amphetamine derivatives possessing powerful hallucinogenic properties, produced splendid psychopharmacological "highs" without experiential density or perception distortion.

A succession of highs was used to intensify self-awareness while controlling simultaneous anxiety. Though the emotional and mental state produced was, of course, artificial—chemical and temporary—the patient experienced a keen "present reality" without the blockage of the neurotic elements, while at the same time evoking comparative anxiety-fraught but "unreal" periphery co-existents consisting of visually manifest recall and re-lived repressed material, usually early traumata.

The patient, in other words, while verbalizing, was able to "watch" and experience a succession of memo-ries, images, and phantasies with his eyes closed, virtual-ly filmlike, as if projected on a screen in a darkened mov-ie theatre.

Since the appearance of blood had twice now preced-ed the manifestation of the chauffeur (Jamie's pillow the first time, and, weeks later, her pierced palm in the Tree Room), Christine ultimately was foolish enough to make a magical connection. And although the idea seemed so outright "insane" she didn't dare tell Dr. Ellenbogen, even managing to squeeze it out of the flood of images when it appeared in one of her ES, or "screen therapy," sessions, she felt compelled to test its possibility.

Concealing a sharp kitchen paring knife in the back pocket of her jeans, she went to the summerhouse, since this commanded a clear and unobstructed view of the en-tire driveway as it wound up to and away from the house—and cut the inside of her forearm with the tip of the blade, avoiding the pale faintly blue branched fork-ing of an artery.

When no blood appeared, though she'd felt the sting of the incision, she pressed the flesh between thumb and forefinger; a drop of it oozed up, shaping itself into a tear that traced a wet path to her wrist.

Then she waited: three minutes, five, the smile of dis-appointment already frozen on her face.

Of course, nothing appeared: neither splendid chauffeur nor long black limousine looming out of the foggy distance. She could no more "make it happen" than she could pluck a flower fully blooming from its closed green bud.

"Obagata," Christine said. "Obagata . . . utagoomba."

"*What?*"

Dr. Ellenbogen leaned closer to the drug-rapt girl. The words had sounded vaguely Swahilian. "*What?*"

"Obagata utagoomba."—Many times, repeated over and over, in a chant.

Good heavens! If the doctor knew anything about languages, it was more shamanistic—straight out of the rainforests of South America, where she had once been herself. Apparently it was a fragment of language the girl had learned from the natives as a child.

"Can you translate; can you say it in English?"

"*Obagata . . .*"

Apparently not. "How old are you, Christine. How old?"

". . . *Utagoomba.*"

"Christine—What is your age? You must tell me."

"*Obagata utagoomba. Obagata . . .*"

Again and again. There was no stopping her.

It seemed part of a ritual, a native dance, one she had watched many times, perhaps even danced herself, whatever her age. How often she had mentioned that she'd played with and imitated the behavior of various tribal children!

By the cadence, the rhythmic quality the girl gave it, the small jerks of her entire body, the doctor could virtually *hear* the heavy beat of the accompanying *dbado* drums, and the wailing flutelike treble of the *kiki-koto,* *see* the sparks swirl from the raging fire, a hundred bleached skulls impaled on poisoned spears; yes, and the ancient shaman in his long coat of blood-dyed feathers and hideous death mask, the stick-thin, ulcer-scarred legs encased in ragged snakeskin, the arthritic joints swollen twice their size, his chest a birdcage under sagging skin smeared bright with blue clay, the withered genitals jouncing and jostling amid countless amulates of tinkling, rattling crocodile teeth, dried toads, and lizard tongues as he hopped and foamed and jabbered and jeered . . .

TWO

Some of her old strangeness was coming back:
the pre-Michael fugues she had experienced in the
months immediately following her father's death, the
lassitude, the postures, the not so painful but irritating
and curious "circular" headaches, as if she were crowned
with thorns, together with hands that ached, palms that
itched and throbbed.

Perhaps it was the beginning of some strange tropical
disease, the germs of which had been dormant and sleeping in her blood.

And with all of this came the compulsive walking
through room after room, miles of walking with undersea
and theatrical slowness, as if the house were a museum of
art or natural history, filled with the artifacts of an ancient civilization that she was seeing for the first time.

Added to this was the endless staring into (usually full-length) mirrors with the sensation of looking at the image of a mysterious stranger, wondering who it was.

This was the "other" feeling, and sometimes a touch of vertigo and double vision went with it. If it was too severe, she had to try to remind herself who she was.

"I am Christine," she said aloud, walking through the rotting rooms in the empty part of the house, the delicate silk of her gown floating behind her with the trailing, fluid grace of a sea anemone.

"I am Christine Kouris; I live in this house. I have a husband whose name is Michael, and two children I call Jamie and Rose . . ."

The strains of *L'Enfance du Christ* reverberated from cellar to attic, making the windows rattle and all the artifacts in the museum tremble.

Playing in the orchard, poking holes into the webbed walls of a huge nest of tent caterpillars they had found, the children heard the music faintly and looked at each other in disgust.

"She's got *that* thing on again," Rose said. "I wish I had some cotton for my ears."

"M-me, too," Jamie agreed, squashing an insect to watch its green entrails ooze out.

Could particles, molecules, atoms of the drug Dr. Ellenbogen was giving her, hide in her body "unmetabolized" and then seep into her blood, crowd into the cells of her brain, making her walk through the world as she would at the bottom of the sea?

Yesterday, she had relived hours of her childhood. It was during the Amazon safari, the Kooma tribe when she was nine, and for sustained moments she had actually *seen* her father on the incredible tridimensional "screen" that defied explanation. It wasn't "out there" before her eyes like a screen in a theatre; rather, it enveloped and permeated her, merging subjective and objective, giving the images she evoked a shocking reality. And there stood her father, flesh and blood, in the glaring triangle of the tent "door," his face shadowed but very clear, the inky eyes snapping with pleasure, the white even-toothed grin making her heart leap into her throat with the joy of having him back, his crushing arms about her, two days earlier than expected.

I am Christine Kouris; I live in this house . . .

She was now in the attic room, the sound of the music deafening; she reached and clicked off the machine. The silence, by sharp contrast, seemed just as loud, crashing over her aching head in a wave.

I have a husband named Michael, and two children . . .

She stared into the standing full-length mirror beside the dress manikin. Ten minutes later, she was still staring motionless into the mirror.

And two children I call Jamie and Rose . . .

She became aware of the pain intensifying in her hands, and, feeling it, thought she heard the crunch of pebbles in the driveway; but when she rushed to the round porthole window, there was no one below. The sound had been in her head. She was disappointed, depressed.

I am Christine Kouris . . .

For the first time, she noticed that the window was screened. Good heavens!—silly Michael! He hadn't neglected even the attic; he'd had every window in the house screened, so afraid was he of "the plague of moths."

On the sill outside, five or six dead ones were lying— their demise a final result of their suicidal efforts to get in.

Actually, they *were* most peculiar, and seemed to infest the whole of the countryside. But, unlike Michael, Christine, who liked insects anyway, found she had absolutely no fear of them; indeed, she had a wonder touched with affection and curiosity.

Oddly, when Michael was at home, even at night, there were few around, but when he was absent, in town shopping, attending to one or another of his sexual needs, perhaps visiting colleagues, the insects, coincidence or not, were clustered at the windows by the hundred come twilight, even earlier on dark and cloudy days, their soft furred bodies thudding blindly against the screens.

More than anything that had occurred or was occurring, the insects were a source of revulsion and bewilderment to Michael. Returning from the village, he would instantly, if he found them about, storm into the house and out again, armed with a broom and several cans of spray insecticide, killing all he could reach, sweeping the dead and semi-dead into black piles of broken wings and bruised bodies.

With stifled cries and shudders, Michael shoveled them into large green plastic trash bags. This done, he would look at Christine with haunted, outraged eyes, virtually accusing her of *complicity* with the insect world in his absence when, of course, she was really quite innocent and as much a victim as he.

At night, when he slept, and if she remained awake, and there was enough moonlight to see, the moths became particularly numerous, covering the screens so densely they became living curtains.

Occasionally, if Michael had taken his valium and slept very soundly, Christine would creep to the downstairs door and, out of intense curiosity, let a number of them in.

When she did so, first opening the door a crack, their behavior was fantastic, the sound of them a muted roar as a horde clustered to the opening, frenzied to be among the privileged few dozen she would allow to enter.

After she'd done so, and if by chance they numbered fifty or so, they seemed to *know*, en masse, exactly what they wanted, or at least, so strangely, what "to do." They would instantly attach themselves, while "weaving" their bodies and wings together in an intricate "fabric" to some part of her body. If she was naked, they might cover a breast or a buttock, perhaps a whole forearm, looking quite, to Christine's pleasure and disbelief, like a sleeve!

They rested so lightly on her skin she had no sensation of their being there at all, but they were so strongly nested and enmeshed, wings, legs, bodies, antennae interlocking securely, that she could literally pull at the "sleeve"—moving it either up or down! Only when she tried to take it off entirely would they break up and, a flutter of separate entities, rise in a cloud, to cluster back again moments later, covering another part of her body.

She was so entertained she had to laugh, and so began the newest of games, for while Michael slept, she could not often resist the persistent, astonishing behavior of the moths.

And just as she had tried to make a magical connection, however unsuccessful, between the appearance of blood and the chauffeur, even to the point of deliberately wounding herself, so she also thought to connect the chauffeur and the moths. She remembered seeing many of them whirl around his head until, annoyed, he'd plucked one from the air, crushing it to fragments.

So, in her intense curiosity, her reckless, childish game-playing desire to bring her own intuited, profoundly longed for but still concealed and mysterious future to its full flower and fruition, temptation soon became compulsion: she opened the door to the moths a bit wider each night.

THREE

As the twin hallucinogens harmaline and ibogaine (MDA-MMDA for short) crept into Christine's brain, seeping through a spiderweb of capillaries into the nuclei of remote and secret cells, her ES (again, "screen" or "field" of internal vision on which she could report) expanded.

The experience, though now familiar, remained as thrilling as anything she had ever known in her life: not because of the enhanced experiential "now" on which the doctor seemed to dote as the primary therapeutic achievement but because of the fantastically "real" quality it gave to memory.

Essentially, the drugs were "time eliminators"; they could delete huge segments of it while also destroying its linear "structure."

Consequently, although memory remained operative, the sense of "being there" was greatly magnified because of the proximity of the now-self to the earlier event. One was not separated by months or years, but, if ideal, by moments: any event in the past, however remote, became virtually "present tense."

"I am seven years old," Christine told Dr. Ellenbogen.

She was lying on the couch with her eyes closed, watching her ES objectively in order to comment and describe. When she chose, or at the doctor's request, she *became* herself as she *saw* herself, but since communication and description were necessary, particularly if she was to regress to preverbal ages, as indeed she might if and when the material demanded it, what she did was tantamount to what a narrator or commentator does for a documentary film or travelogue.

"I am lying on my bed, which is a folding army cot. I wear no clothes at all, except, like a native child, a bright fringed sweatband of dried *ajuta* grass around my head.

"It is intensely hot and humid; I am uncomfortable and cannot sleep although it is well toward midnight.

"We are eight days into the rainy season and already there is an acrid stench of mildew and rot in the air.

"I wear sandals in the daytime since my feet are sensitive and not at all thick-skinned and calloused like the native children, but two nights ago when I left them at the foot of my bed, I woke to find them absolutely furthick—every inch covered with mildew and decay.

"My father told me to rub them with *tanta,* which is a bean oil, but since I could not find any in the native *bures* yesterday, I used some rancid butter, thinking any fat or oil might do.

"As a result, the sandals almost vanished!"—and Christine laughed a little. "This morning they were fifty yards from the tent, being carried off by a river of rave-

nous army ants who apparently thought they had found
two giant delectable cadavers!"

When the to-her humorous quality of the lived-now
memory faded, she continued.

"I am restless and anxious and toss on my bed. I look
up toward the ceiling where a lighted lantern swings, and
can see that the long poles of the tent near the top are already covered with a thick blue-green effulgence, the air-
borne spores of a peculiar fungus having, days ago, with
the beginning of the rain, settled and begun their rapid
growth."

Christine's unusual use of the word "effulgence" as
well as any number of uncharacteristic words did not go
unnoticed by the doctor. However, it was in no way surprising, since most patients gained fluency and increased
facility in their diction under MDA-MMDA because it
exposed and made available for use even unconsciously
acquired vocabulary, apparently stimulating remote language areas of the brain.

She continued describing the "effulgence of fungus,"
revealing that "soon the natives will be carefully scrap-
ing it away wherever it is found because when mature, it
develops minute effluvian blossoms that cough an invisible perfumed vapor into the air, which, though not poi-
sonous in itself, produces pronounced lethargy, and
sometimes sleep so profound that if the sleeper is not
roused, he dies of accelerated dehydration, the flesh rapidly drying out and withering like a mummy's.

"The natives call it *tama-bura,* or "forgetting scent," or
sometimes *tapu-kakakoura,* which is impossible to translate, but combines the idea of 'the shrinking death' with
'the forbidden sleep.'

"In small varied quantities, mixed with certain herbs
and plant extracts which only the shaman seems privy to,

tapu-kakakoura becomes a strong intoxicant as well as an anesthetic which the natives use for circumcision, and also as an aphrodisiac for any of their fertility rites when prolonged sexual arousal and activity are required."

Christine paused to moisten her lips and then went on.

"The sound of the rain beating steadily on the long stretches of canvas (there are several large tents strung together and connected like contiguous rooms) is almost deafening if one listens, but it has gone on for so long and continuously without a single second's respite that it becomes the background against which one lives, and after prolonged exposure, one simply doesn't hear it, though it does sometimes take its toll in ragged nerves, short tempers, even occasional flares of rage and violence that result in murder. If it erupts in this fashion, the natives call it *manikii-ko*, literally 'exploding from the rain.'

"After eight days of it, I myself do not hear the rain, but I do hear the sound of a shovel. It is my father digging outside the tent. The drainage ditches have become clogged, or perhaps they were made too shallow initially; either way, they are filled with water and overflowing so that the slatted wooden platform of the tent floor is completely covered."

Christine's eyes open momentarily, entirely without pupils, totally white, and then gradually close.

"I hear the shovel strike a stone. There is grunting and explosions of breath; evidently it is big and heavy as it is lifted away. I hear my father's voice as he speaks to the natives. He speaks their language perfectly as he is able to speak any language he encounters after just a few days' exposure; he is tremendously gifted that way, with phenomenal memory and ability, even though he had no formal education whatsoever.

"I hear some laughter and scuffling; perhaps they are

making jokes, hitting and pushing each other playfully. The natives adore my father. Principally because, as with any tribe we visit or live with, he literally *becomes* one of them—as if he'd been born of them and knew intimately all their customs and habits.

"He even eats, without variation, everything they eat, no matter how strange. Just before the rainy season, there is one day every year, a few hours really, for the swarming of the termites, or white ants—*tikidonga,* it is called—and they are considered a great delicacy. I saw my father eat them, with the others—living, flying, crawling—by the hundred, brushing, stuffing them into his mouth as they massed over his face. They always come in such incredible numbers that one must wear a netting over one's face if one prefers to breathe properly. Indeed, if forgotten and unattended, many infants have been known to be killed by the termites, literally smothered to death.

"I ate a few myself, to see what they were like, and because my father urged me, but they had no particular taste that appealed to me."

Christine shifted her position, crossing and uncrossing her legs, scratching each palm alternately and so vigorously that both became red. Whether the girl was troubled by a genuine physical irritation or the gesture had a symbolic meaning the doctor was unable to determine. However, soon the motion stopped as the narration continued.

"Not only does my father eat what the natives eat, he also sleeps with them frequently, in groups, both men and women, which is their custom, and joins them in whatever sexual behavior is habitual to them, and enjoyed. My father is immensely sexual—in every way I can think of, in any way I can name. He is so sexual that *ordi-*

nary sex is naive to him, or perhaps I should say incidental and routine—as commonplace and thoughtless as breathing or sneezing."

The doctor interrupted.

"In this context—of sexual behavior—do you speak of your mother?"

The question seemed startling to Christine. She struggled as if unable to get the idea of "mother" into her head. Then—

"No, no. I speak of the natives: countless women; many men; children, too, if it was customary and not taboo. I was positive he was in sexual congress of some sort with the shaman himself, who was a *hideous* man, but possessing much *lekimoko-i,* which is—how shall I say it?—supernatural powers. He could talk to the dead as easily as I am talking to you; and heal wounds in a matter of hours; yes, I have seen it happen; and he could un-possess you very quickly if you were possessed—which virtually everyone was, at one time or another. There seemed to be a population of demons as numerous as the natives themselves. This particular rite is called *ijii-ii*— isn't that funny?—I remember laughing when I first heard it because it sounded more like a sound, a cry, than a word. Then I discovered that it *was* a cry"—and now Christine mouthed it, drawing the sound of it out in a long shuddering wail: *"iiiiiiiiijjjjiiiiiiiiiii!*—like that" while Dr. Ellenbogen's arms were covered with gooseflesh.

"It is a demon's cry," Christine explained; "that is the sound he makes when he is forced by the shaman to leave the body he is trying to own.

"However, I was never possessed, or my father, either. I don't know why. Certainly we were quite as exposed as anyone else. But I suppose the natives, being more primitive, were somehow more *open:* the demons could more easily get in.

"Anyway, I was a bit surprised about my father and the shaman: I mean he was so *unendurably* ugly; and so old you would think he was incapable of *any* kind of sexuality. And perhaps I was mistaken. But I do know that my father several times spent three whole days and nights in his elaborate *bure,* and many times the aphrodisiac variation of the *tapu-kakakoura* was made in a fire outside and brought in to the two of them.

"Of course, my father was there to engage in various and dreadfully secret shamanistic rituals and rites—to *learn,* to acquire shamanistic power himself. But sometimes it was frightening to listen to; because I heard, it seemed, many voices, or several, and finally one that was so unearthly and eerie I knew it couldn't be the shaman's voice or my father's, and no one else was in the *bure.*

"I was sure they had conjured up something fantastic between the two of them: a spirit, a demon, a native god, an entity—I couldn't guess what; I didn't know at first, not until later, but to know my father was to know he was capable of anything, good and bad.

"He had energy beyond belief, health, and superb well-being that virtually radiated from his skin. He was handsome, incredibly handsome always—and was one of those men who grew even more so with the years, until finally, I must admit, it became an embarrassment; yes, if we were in a city, he could not walk a street but that wide-eyed women followed him, some secretly exposing their breasts. And in crowded restaurants, the bars and casinos, men pressed themselves to him: passive, velvet-eyed sodomites, and others, drawn irresistibly to touch any part of him they could find, particularly his genitals, pretending with veiled sly looks and carefully stam-

mered apologies that it had been an accident. He was
never annoyed. He denied no one, embraced everything,
all he could endure without completely exhausting his
nature, even sexually aroused children who, boldest of
all and without thought of disgrace or arrest, threw themselves laughing into his arms, hungry for his mouth, his
hands, his body.

"His appetite for experience, new experience, any experience was insatiable. He seemed to devour, to incor-
porate everything in sight—and forever demand more, always more. All the things in the world were never
enough. *This* world wasn't enough. Knowledge, esoteric
knowledge, and power, these were his passion, his raison
d'être, his sole pursuit."

She was silent a moment, then her eyes opened, rolling
like clouded stones before the lids fell over them again.

"Have you heard of Faust?"

The childish question was quite simple and sincere.
The doctor smiled, answering, "yes"—almost adding, "I
was married to him once"—remembering the detached,
irritating man, the second of four husbands, whom she
had once accused in a stormy, pre-separation argument of
"having no soul."

She suppressed the joke, but instantly gave rise to
another.

"But Faust was a man who exchanged his *soul* for
knowledge; are you suggesting that your father did
that?"

Christine laughed, genuinely amused.

"My father's soul?" The tone was edged with derision.
"Good heavens, no! What could he possibly have done
with that!? Not his soul! . . . but—"

And suddenly, startlingly, the girl was shuddering and
writhing on the couch like an epileptic, the head thrown
back, bubbles of thick saliva covering her mouth, the

tongue protruding and folding back on itself so dangerously that Dr. Ellenbogen feared the girl would swallow
it.

With nothing suitable handy, she quickly stuck the
knuckle of her own doubled forefinger between the girl's
teeth.

Christine bit down very hard, almost drawing blood,
her whole body shaking violently, then suddenly let go
and relaxed, quite as before.

The doctor reached for a tissue and dried the girl's
mouth. The small crisis was over, but the drugs had been
almost two-thirds metabolized. They were utilized by the
body as a predigested glucose in their final stages, the
"high" they produced becoming a pleasant, drowsy feeling of drifting peace and relaxation.

The doctor raised Christine's eyelid to find only a cres-
cent edge of violet pupil barely visible. So there was a little time left, and she planned to make good use of it.

One important and to the doctor potentially fascinating
area had barely been touched, no less explored, Christine
either by truth or design providing little or no information.

"In all this—*where* is your mother?" Dr. Ellenbogen
asked the seven-year-old.

"I don't know," Christine replied faintly; "she isn't
here."

"I would like you to find her. Will you try?"

She raised her voice, speaking louder and somewhat
dramatically, as if making sure the audience at the back
of a large auditorium would not have to strain to hear:
"Where is Clarissa Damenian?" Then she lowered her
tone, speaking intimately: "Do you call her 'Clarissa,' or
'Clara,' or 'Mother,' or what?"

"I call her nothing. She isn't here."

"Dear child— She has to be *some*where. Everyone has a mother. Clarissa Damenian was yours. I take it she's not in your future at the moment. Did you look?"

"Yes."

"Then she must be behind."

"I don't see her. Not from here."

"Can you see a grave or a tombstone anywhere?"

"No."

"Perhaps she was buried at sea."

"No."

"Do you see *any* woman, incidentally, who may have taken her place—in your father's affections, a surrogate mother, so to speak."

"No."

"Then there's only Clarissa. We must find her. Go back; keep going back until you do. It might help if you called her. Do try."

Christine called several times, first "Clarissa," then "Mother," feeling foolish and self-conscious with the unaccustomed words.

"I feel silly," she said. "I know it's useless. It's like knocking on a door when you know no one is there."

"Well, then, go back as I told you. It's always easier that way. Eventually, someone will hear you knocking and open the door. Be five; be four; be three, and *then* look; and be quick before your ES fades. We have made fine progress today. Let's not spoil it. Let's finish off with something . . . triumphant. I want to meet Clarissa Damenian. Christine—Do you hear?"

"Yes."

"How old are you now?"

"Six months."

"Good! Fine! What are you doing?"

Christine had to look deeply into her ES; light was

dimming, edges being blurred. She made an effort to clear things.

"*I* am doing nothing. Someone is changing me because I am wet."

The doctor was pleased.

"Who is it?"

"I can't see. I'm lying on my stomach." Then: "Ah— now I'm on my back, all powdered and dry."

The doctor's excitement grew. "Is it your mother? Is it Clarissa?"

"If it is," Christine replied, always able to joke, "she is black. It is Noonotka. I see the ring in the side of her nose."

"Oh, good heavens!—not *another* native! I am getting weary of those. *Where* is your mother? She must be somewhere. Surely, it must be obvious to you that she *has finally* to appear."

It was so outrageous and indefensible that the girl should calmly and with conviction reply: "I don't think so. No."

It angered the doctor. "I will find her," she promised, "if we have to break up time into weeks, hours, days, minutes!—even if we return you to the womb! Now I insist. Go back, Christine. Back!"

She waited patiently several minutes, then watched with satisfaction as the girl finally began to rock herself gently on the couch like an infant.

"How old are you, Christine?"

"I am three months old."

"What is happening?"

"I'm being fed."

"A breast or a bottle?"

"A breast."

The doctor felt her time of triumph approach; it was

imminent, and in a moment of totally lapsed consciousness, smoothed her hair into place in anticipation of
meeting Clarissa Damenian.

"Whose breast are you nursing?"

"I don't know. I'm not able to see the face."

The doctor had to wait until the feeding was over, but
alas the nipple was black, the breast was black, and, of
course, the white-toothed face grinning down at the
well-fed infant was black too. It was *another* of the natives—this time a wet nurse.

"Where, *where* is Clarissa?" the doctor demanded.

The relived feeding had so enraptured Christine that
she was unable to separate her then-self into her now-self
on her ES, and for a few moments gurgled and cooed on
the couch, ending with a series of small burps.

But the doctor was merciless.

"Back, back!" she insisted, and when Christine's now-
self repossessed her then-self: "How old are you?"

Slowly, faintly: "I am two weeks old . . . I am
one . . . Oh, now! I am two days old . . ."

So with the final turn of the screw: *"Back, back!"* Dr.
Ellenbogen barked.

"Oh!" cried Christine, for she was now but a day old,
and then only hours. "My ES is warping and dim. I am
fading . . ."

"Hold to it! I insist! How old are you? Where is Clarissa?"

"She's not here. There *is* no Clarissa! Oh! I am an hour
old. I am twenty minutes. Oh . . . ! Five . . . two . . .
one!"—and a wailing birth cry welled up from the depths
of Christine's body. In the next few moments, she struggled, curled up in a fetal position, and froze.

Relentless—*"Back!"* the doctor cried; then, fearing she
had lost the child: "Christine—?"

"Yes?" Her ES was still operating; it was her now-self answering, still regressed.

"How old are you?"

"I am minus fifteen seconds. My head has emerged. My father is pulling me out by the shoulders."

"Your father is delivering you?"

"Yes. He is cutting me out of something that is bloody and inanimate."

"Good God! Is your mother dead? Is it a postmortem birth?"

Christine hesitated, her eyes blinking slowly, the pupils half-visible. The drugs had almost worn off.

"I don't know," she murmured. "How can I say? The cry of my birth seems to follow or is mixed with the cry of my mother's death. The moment he took me from her, he killed her."

—Which was indeed surprising news to Dr. Ellenbogen. It took her some moments to recover. Sobered, she had to remind herself that one does not quarrel with history.

She permitted herself one final question.

"Why did he kill her? Do you know?"

"Why not?" was the measured, whispered reply. "She was useless. Her work had been done. *I* was the only thing that mattered: and I had been delivered—" with a look and a sigh of almost drowning ecstacy—"into my father's arms."

The Trunk

I lower the flames of my chandelier, I throw myself on my bed, and turning toward the darkness, I see you, O my daughters, O my Queens!

ONE

THERE CAME A TIME, of course, when not only did
Christine *see* the chauffeur but the chauffeur *saw* Christine.

It was an early evening in late July, when the scent of
honeysuckle in the warm, darkening air was so delicate
and pleasing that Christine, for the sheer pleasure of it,
wandered aimlessly in the twilight—a long leisurely
walk winding around the house, through the orchard,
and back again.

Faintly, as she passed the open front door, she could
hear the slow peck, peck of Michael's typing in his study,
and fainter still, the mingling of music and voices from
the children's TV as they sat on the floor in their bedroom
watching a Western.

She frequently hesitated to come out, because the
moths, once she appeared, especially in the early evening, were sometimes intolerable. They seldom touched

her as she walked, but a whole cloud of them would spin about her head, or, in a whispering funnel of fluttering wings, swirl along behind her.

Tonight, however, there were very few: only three or four darting about rather aimlessly: this, being most unusual, filled her with anticipation: the evening promised to surprise her with novelty, something unexpected.

She wasn't wrong. But there was no crunch of pebbles this time; he and the car with its open door were already "there": suddenly—like a "cut" shot in a film—just as she rounded a corner.

And seeing him, and this time he her, her heart began to pound with discovery and delight, because however subtle, *he'd* been startled, too; yes!—she'd not missed his small quick step backward to retain his balance, the sudden rapid jerk of his head the moment she'd "materialized" out of the twilight around the ruined northern wing of the house.

How astonishing that he should have been surprised!—when he had looked for her so often, through almost all of the early summer; how they had looked for *each other*, really, for the failure of the first knife had not discouraged her: there had been other knives at other impatient times, the idea of a magical connection remaining obsessive and persistent.

Ah, now, but here he was!—no knife required, apparently—(how could she have been so wrong, bleeding herself senselessly, so often?)—his head motionless, his eyes full upon her, his whole body in its stance, its manner, its posture and attitude, speaking of delayed recognitions.

He had found what he'd sought and, unless she was mistaken, the corners of his wide handsome mouth were upturned in pleasure.

If she'd had to think about it—this longed for encounter—she wouldn't have known what to do next, but there was no need to think at all. She was an actress in a play she had written herself and rehearsed a thousand times, knowing the role so well no thought was involved at all, indeed would have confused her. She simply had to wait for her cue, and then, without effort, perform. The car was waiting, the door was open.

She wasn't really close to him; nevertheless, never had she seen him so clearly; not quite his face (though he *was* smiling, *surely* he was smiling!), which remained for a time a pale handsome blur, but if there had been the tiniest wrinkle, the merest micron of dust on his uniform, she knew she would have been able to see it.

It was quite as if her eyes had the power of a film "zoom" camera: able to move in for very close views or pull back as far as she chose. Consequently, as he removed the black leather gloves from his hands, her eyes were inches from his fingers: they were square-tipped, strong, the skin marble smooth, the nails immaculate and perfectly shaped; below the starched, almost glaring-white of his cuffs, the short glossy black hairs on his wide-boned wrists could be seen.

Then, as with languid ease, he tossed the gloves into the front window of the car behind him, her eyes adjusted to provide a head-to-toe view of the whole, lean, ranging length of him, before her vision moved in very close once more.

Now his ghostly face filled everything she could see, crowding into her. Then the mouth opened to a round blurred blackness, closed, opened again, light from somewhere catching the point of a tooth that flashed a pinpoint as brilliant as a firefly.

Good God, he had spoken!—twice, two words; but the lips were out of synch! It *still* wasn't time. And in a dream-void, she waited for the deep, elongated sound of the two words to reach her: her name.

"Chhhhhhhhhhrrrrrrrrrrrrrriiiiiiiiiiissssssssssstiiiiiiiiinnnne!
Chhhhhhhhrrrrrrrrrriiiiiiiiiiissssssstiiiiiiiiiiinnnnnnnnnne!"

TWO

CHRISTINE HADN'T BEEN WRONG about the knives; at least, not about the blood.

When the reality of the chauffeur had faded and she saw only a few gnarled trees that began the labyrinth of the apple orchard beyond the pebbled drive where he had stood against his car, she felt an aching strangeness and a wet warmth in the palms of her hands.

If she didn't know what it *meant,* she was totally aware of what it *was.* Both palms were pierced, quite as if she'd been crucified! Was it possible, at all possible, that unknowingly she had done it to herself? She looked at the small tear-shaped wounds, bewildered, but not entirely surprised. After all, if not this, she had expected *something.* But how could she possibly explain it to Michael?

She couldn't. She wouldn't. He simply must never know.

149

* * *

Michael found out about his wife the very next day. She came into the kitchen at breakfast time with her hands grossly bandaged, and when he demanded the reason, she pretended that she had burnt herself at the stove the night before "heating milk" to make her sleeping pills "work better."

—Which was possible, Michael supposed, until he saw the pink blush in the white gauze centered in each of Christine's palms. Burns, unless they were extremely severe, didn't bleed.

It took more than a half-hour and a final raging, shouting display of Michael's temper to get the bandages off so he could have a look, and perhaps, if need be, take her to a doctor.

So, at the point of exhaustion and, what was worse, thoroughly bored and finally indifferent, Christine gave in and watched a profoundly shocked and truly stupid expression glaze Michael's entire face as he knelt before her, unfastened the bandages, and stared open-mouthed at her hands.

When the silence and his dumb look became finally intolerable, she said: "Maybe I'm a saint. Do you think? You didn't know that about me, did you," adding, "And it isn't even Easter."

Michael was so numb he went along with the incredibly bad joke. "If it happens at all," he replied, "it happens on Good Friday. And never in America. Always . . . in some thoroughly remote village in— *Bavaria*, I believe." He looked into her eyes. "Since you've lived *everywhere*—by your own unsolicited admission—have you ever lived *there*, by any chance?"

Christine shook her head: somehow the tiniest, the naughtiest of little girls.

"Not in Bavaria. Never there."

"Ah," Michael replied, "then this couldn't have happened by *proxy* so to speak. I mean, you didn't *imagine* you were back there, lying on a bed of straw, without a scrap of food for forty days, sharing identity, delirious with dreams of the final hours of agony of your Lord . . . ?

"No," Christine murmured, truly frightened of Michael's severe manner, which resembled the most dreadful of criminal lawyers cross-examining a hostile witness.

But he was making a wicked, taunting, mocking, even sadistic joke, of course, because she knew he couldn't believe she'd done it herself *to* herself.

She was wrong. It was, to him, *her* version of *The Passion Play*, and another and this time monstrous symptom of her astonishing illness: *self-mutilation*, or, perhaps, *symbolic* self-mutilation, however inaccessible and mysterious the symbolic meaning and character of it remained at the moment.

"Well, if your *dreams* didn't crucify you, my darling, what *did*? Or is that like asking a leper why his fingers are falling off?" He was making a mockery of loving, sympathetic patience, and concern. "Could you be troubled for an explanation?"

Her absolutely wide- and clear-eyed sincerity made her answer difficult to doubt, her look containing as much innocence as Eve's must have to Adam the first time she saw him.

"I have none. It just—" a swallow "—happened."

"Like the wind," Michael said with a sweet evil smile; "—like the rain, and the sunshine . . . "

"Yes," Christine agreed softly. "—Like those."

And in the next shocking moment he was on his feet, shouting and stomping about maniacally.

"Oh, no! No, my dearest, my darling! *Not* like those at all! More like *thousands* of ghastly black moths, and a treeful of *murdered* starlings . . . *lakes* of blood, and locked *trunks*, and *ghostly* chauffeurs opening car doors, and more like . . . " It didn't fit with the others but he included it anyway: "—More like *lascivious* women . . . *lewd* naked girls atop their hills, waving seductively to *lusting* milkmen at unearthly hours of the morning . . . !"

He was being shockingly, irresistibly funny, and Christine exploded in laughter—itself so infectious that Michael was helpless to do anything but join her.

Together they doubled over, virtually rolling on the floor. Living with her so long was apparently teaching him to be an actor, too, and a playwright sometimes as lunatic as she. What he had done just now was to provide what the tragic, horrifying, but finally boring seriousness of the moment required: a bit of comic relief.

But after they had laughed their laughter, two grisly facts remained.

"They've stopped bleeding," Christine said. "And they don't hurt."

She examined the wounds closely with profound curiosity, then held her hands at arms' length toward the windows.

"Look, Michael!" she said monstrously; "you can see the light through the holes!"

The pun that occurred to Michael was hideous, but hideous puns exist, and he was its author. The moment he saw the light through Christine's palms, he indeed "saw the light"—which was that this incredible woman, this incurably bizarre and fantastically ill girl (no matter *what* Dr. Ellenbogen considered "progress"—begging

his patience, expecting her prognosis to be as fascinating
to him as it was to her) could no longer be the mother of
his children.

He would go to the employment agencies this very
week, advertise in the local newspapers if necessary, inquire among his friends (and sexual partners), begin in-
terviewing as soon as possible, and install someone sane
and motherly in the house by late summer, certainly before his classes resumed in the fall.

Yet every time his mind turned to a housekeeper, his
initial enthusiasm and determination began as usual to
wane when he thought also of Christine.

Would anyone, *could* anyone (save his own, blind,
adoring, no-matter-what self) put up with this unbeliev-
able woman?—this unaging, violet-eyed, golden-tressed,
child-bodied, heart-stoppingly beautiful girl?—i.e., *monster: self-crucified, paranoiac schizophrenic*: attacked by
starlings, smothered by amorous moths, hallucinating a
seductive, apparently unemployed chauffeur who desired to drive her *God-knows-where-and-to-what* in a
gold-chromed black Rolls-Royce!

A housekeeper was obviously *out*; and Michael's
thought turned to alternatives: harder decisions had to be
made. But one thing; clearly now—Christine and the
children *had* to be separated soon—even if it necessitated
putting Jamie and Rose in a private school, or an institu-
tion, or a foster home.

And with this last depressing possibility—the loss of
his children—acutely paining both heart and mind,
Michael made a peculiar and seemingly unrelated instant
decision: *he was going to open Christine's trunk.*

Decisions are made, and then the reasons for having
made them are thought about and explored, the uncon-

scious being well known for pulling horses with carts.

Also, the subliminal's sense of justice remains primitive, not being as sophisticated and recently acquired as our own. Ask it, and it will still, after so many thousands of years, reply: an eye for an eye, a tooth for a tooth.

So Michael's "justice" was born of the final and dire threat to the children and the potential loss of them to himself, together with a bursting accumulation of years of suppressed anger and smothered rage, rejection, humiliating sexual denial, cruelly spurned gestures of love. —All this, and more: particularly his more recent frustration and disappointment that Dr. Ellenbogen had absolutely failed to improve her patient, and his own continued and unrelieved *appalled* astonishment at Christine's self-indulgence—for however much a "victim" to her strange illness and its variety of unusual symptoms, she was a *willing* victim—self-exposed, inviting—as responsible as the profoundly death-wishing "innocent" who manages so surprisingly and accidentally to stumble in front of the onrushing car.

More simply and practically, the somewhat strained logic went like this: if *she* (Christine) can do all these (rotten) things to me (Michael), then by God *I* can do a few (rotten) things to *her*. For one thing, I can open her precious goddamn trunk. —To balance things. —To make *all* the games more even. —To show her that *I* too, if I choose, am capable of shameful, disgusting, self-indulged, immoral, egomaniacal, life-destroying, love-destroying behavior. —And how does she like it? —Eh?

Once you lusted after this man like a hunter of vampires . . .

The thought sobered Michael.

Is that what the doctor meant by providing him with a

new hammer and stake? Reinvesting him with the energy and spirit the hunt required?

If so, amen. God knows, it was probably much later than he thought. —Too late. Nevertheless, good or bad, regardless of the consequences, whether it completely and finally wrecked his life and career, or—how significant the opposite!—returned his adored wife loving to his arms, he knew he must, *must* smash into her crazy "attic's *attic*," and with crowbar and hammer, and axe if need be, render to shreds and splinters Christine's worshiped trunk, raze it from top to bottom, wantonly spill out its secrets for his probing eyes and seizing fingers to explore.

How often life falls disappointingly short of the imagination.

With Christine at Dr. Ellenbogen's for one of her therapy sessions, Michael arrived at the attic's attic with so many heavy tools and so much bursting determination that he could have opened Ahknaton's tomb without the slightest effort, only to find the padlock hanging loose on its clasp and the door ajar: simple carelessness, no doubt.

He was, of course, disappointed. The whirlwind, so long in the making, and thinking to root up a house, had found only a few dry leaves to spin around idly.

However, the long coffin-shaped trunk under its intricate, richly detailed Persian rug revived his interest. He threw back the cover, his eyes devouring the careful antique workmanship that had combined wood, metal, and leather to make it the handsome, indeed beautiful, trunk it was.

It seemed a pity to force the crowbar into the heavy brass of its two end locks and then the center one, which was shaped into the crude head of an animal or a man with a horned snake emerging from its mouth, but force all three he did without pause or hesitation.

The heavy top moved up with a groaning creak of its hinges, but it must have been springed and weighted, so lightly and effortlessly did it rise.

As it rose, Michael recalled the joke he had made to himself when Christine had insisted that the trunk go with them to Greece after their wedding.

I've married a vampire's daughter, he'd thought; *she's got her father in the trunk!*

And now, looking down into it, at all the things she'd considered so precious, he dropped to his knees aghast, wishing to God it *had been* her father he'd found instead.

. . . No, no; I speak of the natives: countless women, many men; children, too, if it was the custom and not taboo . . .

I was positive he was in sexual congress of some sort with the shaman himself, who was a hideous man, but possessing much lekimoko-i . . .

Dr. Ellenbogen stopped the machine, pressed FF for fast forward, and then listened again, this time picking up Christine's weird imitation of the wail of the possessed as he was being exorcised.

. . . However, I was never possessed; or my father, either . . .

The doctor stopped the tape, toying absently with the controls as she pondered what she'd heard. She touched the volumn knob accidentally, increasing the sound to almost maximum pitch. When she again pressed P for play, she was startled to hear her own voice thunder through the room, rattling and shaking all the objets d'art on the end tables: . . . *Good God! Is your mother dead? Is it a postmortem birth . . . ?*

She quickly lowered the volume, then in a series of backward-forward jumps, kept searching for something Christine had said that now, in retrospect, appeared to be a clue of the greatest importance, yet in the rush of the girl's monologue had slipped by the doctor unheeded instead of being isolated and examined.

. . . *To acquire shamanistic power himself. But sometimes it was frightening to listen to; because I heard, it seemed, many voices, or several, and finally one that was so unearthly and eerie I knew it couldn't be the shaman's voice or my father's, and no one else was in the* bure . . .

. . . *I was sure they had conjured up something fantastic between the two of them: a spirit, a demon, a native god, an entity . . .*

The word "entity" entertained the doctor; what an incredible mind the child had . . .!

. . . *I couldn't guess what; I didn't know at first, not until later . . .*

That was important, of course; the doctor hadn't missed it, and she'd make Christine return to it another time to elaborate. But it wasn't what she wanted at the moment.

So the search continued.

. . . *Women followed him, some secretly exposing their breasts. And in crowded restaurants, the bars and casinos, men pressed themselves to him: passive, velvet-eyed sodomites, and others . . .*

—Forward and backward, and forward again—in pursuit of her prey . . .

. . . *Even sexually aroused children who, boldest of all, and without thought of disgrace or arrest, threw them-*

selves laughing into his arms . . .

. . . He denied no one, embraced everything, all he could endure without completely exhausting his nature . . .

Perhaps she was buried at sea . . .

. . . I was the only thing that mattered . . .

Suddenly, the doctor stayed with the last sentence, listening to it over and over, the quality of it being important, the inflection given individual words. If the sentence had been written, the *I* would have been italicized or in quotes: *"I" was the only thing that mattered* . . . *"I" was the only thing* . . . *"I"* . . . *"I"* . . .

She went back to listen again to the one dreadful reference to Clarissa Damenian:

. . . Her work had been done . . . *She was useless* . . . *The moment he took me from her, he killed her* . . .

It was stunning.

And the doctor smiled, stroking her hair. Still— What she wanted hadn't yet been found, though she felt a sweet anxiety, an implied crisis of imminent discovery.

. . . My father's soul? Good heavens, no; what could he possibly have done with that!? Not his soul! . . . but—"

The "that" of course, referred to Marcus Damenian's "soul." But who was the "he" who could not possibly *do* anything with it?

Suddenly the doctor cut off the machine with a cry of laughter and surprise. How stupid could she be? The ambiguity of a pronoun, of all things, had confused her. Christine wasn't saying "he." She was saying *"He!"*

" . . . My father's soul?—good heavens, no; what could He possibly have done with that . . . ?"

What it amounted to was a deprecating censure of a

prevailing myth. Out of the mouths of babes—a euphemism, if there ever was one, for the deepest unconscious—had come the destruction of the Faust legend.
The astonishing "He" of Christine's phantasmagoria no
longer trafficked in "souls."

His business lay manifestly elsewhere.

THREE

ONCE, WHEN THEY WERE SMALLER, Jamie and Rose
sneaked out of bed at three in the morning to watch a
monster movie on TV.

The huge, staggering creature whose clothes didn't fit,
and who had kind of a square head and shiny bolts on
either side of his neck, was positively hair-raising to see,
but one part, when he played by a lake with a little girl,
wasn't so frightening; indeed, it was rather sad because
he kept moving his mouth, trying to smile, and grunting
at her, imitating what she did with his giant stupid
hands, like a little kid.

Jamie, who thought he had discovered at least one
dreadful secret of the film, pressed his trembling lips
close to Rose's ear, stammering in a whisper, "He c-c-
can't talk!"

His sister looked at him in disdain. "I *know* that! They
forgot to sew in a tongue, and then, after the lightning
made him alive, it was too late."

The monster was now rising, the little girl dead in his arms. He hadn't *meant* to kill her, that was the heartbreaking part, and Rose, tearful herself, had to comfort Jamie, drying his tears, wiping the running wetness from under his nose.

Curiously, and certainly coincidentally—but just like the film in which the monster was created—a bolt of lightning split the black afternoon sky over the apple orchard, and when Jamie and Rose parted the leaves in one of the walls of the Tree Room to see if it had struck anything and maybe, please God, set something afire, they saw instead, standing a few yards away "the man in the black suit."

Because of the lightning and the man's sudden appearance, though he may have been standing where he was for a long time, both Jamie and Rose with synchronized instancy recalled the film and the chained monster being lowered from the spitting, hissing fire of the sky.

But, of course, the man wasn't nearly as tall as the monster, had no shiny bolts on either side of his neck, and his clothes seemed to fit him quite properly.

Jamie suddenly remembered that he had seen him before, just a glimpse, but now, unless he'd simply missed it the first time, the man wore a visored cap; this, together with his black, gold-buttoned uniform, made the child think he was looking at a motorcycle cop, but then he remembered that their suits were dark blue, with silver buttons and a badge.

Rose, having been born five minutes earlier than Jamie, had always been five minutes smarter.

"He's a chauffeur," she announced in a whisper.

"What's that?" Jamie asked.

"Well—"

She didn't know precisely all a chauffeur's duties. "He drives people around. He's a servant, sort of—like the housekeeper Daddy says he's going to get us."

Her attention was drawn back to the chauffeur, who seemed bored with his waiting, shifting his weight, walking a few idle steps.

"Look—! There's his car."

They saw the Rolls for the first time, far to the left, about thirty yards behind him, it being difficult to see because the approaching storm had made the day so inky blue. A heavy ground fog, following a sudden drop in temperature, was beginning to roil in from the orchard. It had already veiled the car, making it appear smoky and unreal.

The chauffeur kept staring about, often up at the house, his head turning this way and that, as if he were keeping an appointment with someone who was late.

"Who does he want?" Jamie whispered.

Rose shrugged. But with the intuition of the primitive and the child, she knew, her heart beating a little faster than usual. She also remembered the day she and Jamie had leaned from the upstairs window, Christine rushing from the door down below with the frantic cry—"did you *see* him?!"

So this was the "him" they hadn't seen.

But Christine was in town for the afternoon—at the doctor's, where she spent one or two hours almost every day, and had to go even more times now, they were told, because she had hurt her hands on the kitchen stove and had to have them fixed.

Hearing no answer, Jamie repeated the question.

Rose replied: "I think he wants *us*." She was jealous,

and anyway always ready to frighten her brother if she could.

But this didn't make sense to Jamie, who knew that adults hated children; and what could a strange man do with two small kids?

"What are all those things around his head?" he persisted, anxious for satisfying information of *some* sort— for small dark objects were slowly spinning about the chauffeur.

"They're *moths*, stupid," Rose replied. "—The ones Daddy hates and keeps killing all the time. They pester *every*one."

At least *that* was something unmysterious with which Jamie could deal with pleasure.

"Oh!" he smiled, pleased. And cupping Rose's ear as if what he said was naughty or a secret: "They keep following Mommy around if she goes out at night. And if *she* sits down, *they* sit on *her!*"

Both of them had now to strangle their laughter, clutching at each other in spasms of hugging desperation to keep their enjoyment quiet so the chauffeur wouldn't hear.

Useless! His searching eyes soon moved to the outside wall of the Tree Room, instantly finding leaves that trembled and branches that shook.

A black-gloved hand beat back a flurry of moths as he sank slowly to his haunches so he could be just the children's height.

All his movements were strangely slow, even the crinkling of his black, shiny eyes, the pale lips parting, the mouth opening in its happy smile of discovery and surprise.

A moth flew right against his teeth, and even the backward jerk of his head was slow; and the lethargic wings of the moth as it spun away seemed timed exactly to meet the hand that seized and crushed it.

He spat, the handsome face furrowed in momentary anger; then all was reasserted: the smile, the discovery, the happy surprise.

He removed his gloves, tucking them into a breast pocket, and stretched one hand outward in the direction of leaves that no longer trembled, branches that no longer shook.

There the hand waited, frozen in air, until Rose, being five minutes braver than her brother, eased her body through the wall of the Tree Room, revealing herself. She reached back and pulled a somewhat reluctant Jamie to her side.

Seeing the two emerge from the leafy wall, the chauffeur remained on his haunches, his hand still invitingly outstretched, his handsome smile broadening. If he wanted Christine, he wanted them also, and with faint, shy grins, they moved slowly toward him.

The man was irresistible, utterly familiar—like a beloved uncle, an adored father: radiating a strong if peculiar kind of love that made them bend quickly toward his mouth, aching to receive his warm and smiling kisses.

Immediately after the heavy brass locks were torn from Christine's trunk and just moments before Michael raised the lid and dropped to his knees, he hesitated, anxiety and a dire premonition of great magnitude seizing him.

An event from the past, so much like the present moment, was flooding his memory.

During the week of his mother's funeral—indeed, on

the very afternoon of the burial, when that incredible sense of desolation, of absence and loss that follows death, settled over the entire house—Michael found the key to the desk where his mother kept her "private" things.

Actually, he had always known where she kept it, and she had known that he knew, apparently never doubting that he'd betray her trust. He never had. What, then, led him to do so after her death? What impelled him?

The nurse had left days ago, his sister was now on the train back to her boarding school, and his father had locked himself in his bedroom for what was to be three days' duration—half in sobbing grief, half in the abundant justification to drink presented to his semi-alcoholic self by his wife's untimely and tragic death.

So Michael was left alone. Entirely. To eat what he found or buy what he wanted. To sleep when he could. Do what he pleased. Alone with the emptiness, the silence, except for the faint, persistent, daylong drone of the heavy spring rain.

"Privacy" is a euphemism to a child. It translates into "secret," and secret often means "magical." Hidden things, kept from profane eyes and touch, acquire potency and power.

All children are phylogenetic primitives. Perhaps Michael sought to resurrect a beloved madwoman—at least re-experience her, lessen his loss by touching, handling, discovering all the secret, magical possessions she kept in her hiding place.

In any event, he opened her desk. Alas. To his sadness, to his exacerbated grief and misery, even disgust, everything he found was quite as dead and foreign, alien and grotesque as the painted dummy they told him was his mother, dressed in jeweled finery and stuffed into a mahogany coffin—the ill-sewn wrists (he had actually peeked) swathed in lace and ringed with silver.

. . . Old postcards; letters, creased and recreased, yellow with age, a few speaking of love and absence, some signed by his father, others not; faded photographs: people in strange clothes he had never seen or knew existed, surely dead long ago; pale ribbons, a pressed flower crumbling under his touch; ancient menus from restaurants in San Francisco, New Orleans, Athens, Rome; announcements to weddings, christenings; black-bordered invitations to view the dead; countless sympathy cards: hundreds of these relating to his brother, lovingly tied in ribbons like ancient love letters; a partial denture, which he handled with mixed horror and fascination; three pairs of eyeglasses, evidently discarded as her vision grew steadily worse; a diaphragm; bottles of all kinds; many small prescription-type containers with pills and capsules of all colors, most of them reading "one or two at bedtime for sleep."

Seconal, nembutal, dalmane, librium, demerol . . . the words meant nothing until years later, the language of a foreign country.

He picked up the diaphragm: this he had no name for, but fingered the strange object with the psychokinetic ease of a talented medium: knowing subliminally exactly what it was, having consciously absolutely no idea. In any event, it repelled him, as did all the dead and useless things he'd found, not one of them magical, or even truly secret, none with powers of resurrection, all of them "junk": pathetic and worthless.

So knowing at last that there was nothing to be known, he locked the madwoman's desk, secreted the key where he had found it, and wandered out into the springtime rain to join April in her weeping.

FOUR

NO TRUTH IS OBJECTIVE; it is a subjective human experience. As such, "truth" came slowly to the kneeling Michael, for though he touched and handled at first timidly, many of the amazing things in Christine's trunk, each had a history and a significance (wedded to shock) that he had to abstract and present to numbed sensibilities and a mind that persisted in remaining incredulous, protectively resistant, and frankly stupid.

What, *what*, for example, was he to make of the fact that Christine was not only a multimillionaire, but a multi-multimillionaire?—perhaps easily a billionaire.

This was the first, the most innocent and acceptable of his discoveries, for occupying a third of the trunk, pushed carelessly to one end, were numerous foot-high, loosely stringed stacks of legal currency, bills, somewhat yellowed and stained with age, of huge denominations, while, more shocking than this, a large plastic bag con-

tained fifty or more bankbooks attesting to truly fabulous
sums of money deposited in banks in Switzerland,
France, Mexico, Argentina—twenty or more countries, as
well as at least a dozen major banking institutions in the
United States. Some were in her own name, but most in
her father's, marked "hold in trust for Christine M.
Damenian."

Michael had to touch the money itself many times, ex-
tracting single bills, holding each to the light of the window that he might observe the minute hair-veins of blue
and red that declared them genuine and not (as his mind
begged him to believe) counterfeit, bogus: stage money
as fake as Christine's junk jewelry, her histrionic exhibi-
tions of costume and dramaturgy. And although he scru-
tinized the bankbooks with equal zeal, comparing signa-
tures, adding columns, observing dates, addresses, ini-
tials, ink stains, smudges—any slight indication of error
or defect that would indicate forgery, fakery, ruse—he
found none.

He sank back on his heels with a glazed, dumb look in
his eyes. There remained no doubt in his mind, none
whatsoever: no matter how in the world such a man as
Marcus Damenian could have amassed it, all this incredible wealth, multiplying itself with every passing minute
in banks all over the world, was *real*, a bequest from her
father, and belonged to Christine.

Fortunately, Michael had looked at the money first.
The effect was so stunning that it became a true hypnotic,
numbing the "feeling" centers of his brain, tranquilizing
his emotions, preparing them sufficiently to bear the infinitely more shocking and astonishing secondary discoveries that awaited his wide eyes and trembling fingers in
other sections of what—in his ignorance and bathos—

he'd had the stupidity to call Christine's *mysterious*
trunk. He was about to learn how much closer he'd been
to the truth when he'd accused her of *horrendous* secrets.
Mr. Kouris—
The memory-voice was Dr. Ellenbogen's, gentle but
with absolute conviction . . .
Mr. Kouris, I assure you—
The memory-face was Dr. Ellenbogen's face, the crinkly mummy-map smiling ever so faintly, leaning close to
his . . .
I assure you there are *photos . . . many photos . . .
somewhere . . .*
He had known *then* where the "somewhere" was, as he
knew *now* that under a cover of palely yellowed linen
wrapped around it, a thick album of photos was but
inches from his fingers, seconds from his eyes. And he
knew also in this briefest of delays before the actual
physical act of looking—for such is the noetic quality of
the mind—what he would see, what he would find.
    And, of course, he found it.
    Among a hundred or more photos in the album, some
quite ordinary, were at least twenty of (unmistakably)
Christine at all ages, from infancy onward, and (presumably) her father, Marcus Damenian, in every imaginable
act and position of physical love and sexual intimacy.

    That a man should make love to his daughter could
hardly have been surprising to Michael, even if the woman in question was now and had been for more than sev-
en years his wife.
    Incest was commonplace, even the norm in some prim-
itive societies, as were most sexual differences, and his
own life had been replete with such a variety of sexual
experiment that in retrospect it probably could have been

considered "unusual." His final strong preference, however, was for rather "normal" heterosexual relationships.

Also, through travel, art, film, anthropological literature, books of all kinds, he knew perhaps all there was to know—or cared to—about variant and deviate sexual behavior.

One of the shocks of his life was seeing for the first time in Korea a peasant woman fellate her infant son. He learned later, and after having witnessed it a number of times throughout the countryside, that it was a common practice—a "sedation" to sooth crying babies, comparable in its effect to the use of a pacifier in Western societies. (And, parenthetically, if in Michael's mind at the time Freud's theory of infantile sexuality was ever in doubt, the sight of countless small erections and contented expressions on the faces of Korean babies under the ministrations of their mothers soon enough demolished it.)

On the whole, Michael considered himself knowledgeable and worldly in such matters, his exposure catholic, his tolerance generous.

Nevertheless, Christine's photos came as a profound shock. He actually trembled and shook, and had to wait to quiet himself before he was able to lift his eyes and study the pictures again.

Then he looked for as long as he could bear—at graphic displays of mouth-genital eroticism when Christine was an infant, to strongly executed full coition when she was an (anatomically) capable child.

What was infinitely worse, he looked for as long as his *own* excitement and incipient arousal would tolerate—for the compounded horror of his own feasted viewing was the knowledge that he *enjoyed* looking at this man-and-infant, man-and-child sexual relatedness and that his own sexual nature, the complexities and mysteries of which he had to the limit of the law and his own conscience indulged but never psychoanalytically explored, was keenly stimulated super-alive with the thrill of vicarious involvement.

He continued to look until, suddenly, he thought he might *throw the cat out the window!*—the bewildering association all but shattering his mind.

Surely the cat *would* go out the window, and *he* after it, if he didn't take his eyes from these particular photos.

He jumped quickly ahead a dozen pages and there, staring up at him, was—good heavens!—what? Surely not Christine at the age of six or seven in a Communion dress! It couldn't be. Michael was sure that the closest Christine had come to any church in the whole of her life was that eternal recording of *L'Enfance du Christ*. Nevertheless, here she was, in frilly white, lace collar, and (medical gauze?) veil, standing next to three naked black children, one with his nose pierced by a splinter of bone.

She carried no prayer book, no rosary was in evidence, so Michael concluded quickly enough that the picture had nothing to do with Communion. No. It was simply one of the earliest examples of Christine's "dress up" occasions, the budding beginnings of her theatrical moods and getups—which, of course, it was. But he was chagrined to realize that it was probably on the basis of such flimsy and totally amateur experiences as this that Christine had had the audacity to tell Dr. Ellenbogen that before her marriage, she'd had an enormously successful "career" in the theatre.

He looked more closely at the photo, a bit puzzled. There was something about Christine's face as depicted: a radiance, a smile both sly and beatific, that made him think her father must have taken the photo; yes; surely she was looking into his face, his eyes, not the camera.

And who had taken the other photos?—the dreadful sexual ones? How strange!—unless a timer had been used—to have had someone there, focusing, making sure there was enough light, while father and daughter apparently "positioned" themselves to their liking. Well, why think of that?—anyone, a native, a servant, could have been the photographer. And knowing Christine's superego-less psychopathic lack of sensitivity about exhibiting herself, he now knew from whom (and what) it had come.

Michael had examined Christine in the photos until he thought his eyes would fall from his head.

But what of Marcus Damenian? Somehow he had managed to look without seeing: denying, at least temporarily, the man's body in the sexual photos: its beauty, its strength, its well-muscled and finely developed athletic quality, the stunningly proportioned and sized genitalia. Now, with the turn of a page, Michael faced with full conscious seeing an eight-by-ten photo of Marcus Damenian's face.

Ah, he thought meanly: Dorian Gray's *father* . . . and laughed a little between rage and weeping, with a flood of hopelessness and despair because the man was so unspeakably handsome.

What had he expected? The Hunchback of Notre Dame?—An evil, twisted, sexually perverted, vile mountebank of visible corruption?

What he got was the calm, faintly smiling, *lovely* face of a young priest about to take his final vows. A marvelous face, really!—and over it, out of it, emanating from it: a ghostly, genetic promise: the exquisite, heart-stopping face that was Christine's.

* * *

There were other photos, but none with the interest of those he had already seen, and, oddly, none of what he had hoped to see: at least one of Christine's mother, Clarissa Damenian.

But jungles?—yes!—many pictures: natives, ceremonies, rituals, circumcisions, dances, marriages, burial rites; and countless animals: alive, dead, hunted, snared, skinned, roasted, eaten. Ah, and not one, but at least ten or twelve of various witch doctors, presumably in their elaborate Sunday-best getups. And the firewalk, yes; that was there, too: naked man and child, hand in hand, in the center of a long white pit over which the air was warped and dancing with heat. But it was disappointing: a very long view, man and child only vaguely seen and slightly distorted, veiled in a haze of smoke and steam. But—if he would make out their faces at all, if he could make them out—both, both were smiling.

What remained in Christine's "mysterious" trunk for Michael's strained, bloodshot eyes to see?

Hadn't he had shock enough?

Well, there was a final one left—the most profound of all, and one which, regrettably, if it did not throw the entire cat out the window, threw at least eight of its nine lives.

But before he got to this final discovery, he had to rummage through and carelessly push aside countless "things" he couldn't possibly truly name: they looked like "junk," and he suspected they might be. If someone with a weak brain had invented a child's game called Voodoo and packaged it like Monopoly, the box might have contained many of the things Michael found: all the ridiculous, tired clichés of the "dark arts": black candles, misshapen dolls, bleached bones, dried—skin?—that looked suspiciously as if it had come from frogs or lizards, many strings of beads that were surely dried navy beans or cranberries, and countless leather, drawstring bags containing . . . he couldn't guess: perhaps the mysterious possibly genuine jungle drugs Dr. Ellenbogen had intimated Christine might possess.

This aside, the rest seemed like the pathetic paraphernalia of a slightly demented six-year-old preparing to scare a few younger siblings on All Hallow's Eve.

Absurdly, Michael imagined there might even be a "magic wand" or a "witch's hat" and was actually looking, digging deeper into the trunk when he came across the final, supreme horror.

From under the piles of bankbooks and money, protruded . . . He closed his eyes, praying for strength to slam down the lid of the trunk that he might never know what he suspected it was. Better to live in agonized doubt than fatal confrontation.

But only a resurrected saint speeding to heaven could have resisted. In the next moment, he'd seized the thing in both hands: a huge, thick, heavily veined and intricately surfaced dildo—kept moist and air tight, apparently, inside its transparent plastic bag—so realistic in its latex modeling or whatever fleshlike imitation that composed its shape and substance, so astonishingly *warm*, so vibrantly *alive* to touch, that Michael had an unendurable, vile excitement, the splendor-disgust of believing, without doubt, that he had seized and handled the blood-pulsing reality of Marcus Damenian's living, moving phallus.

With a croak of loathing, he dropped it back into the trunk and slammed the lid, collapsing over it, his head and stomach pounding in waves of vertigo and nausea.

FIVE

Put-put . . .

Put-put-put . . .

It was Christine driving back from the doctor's, the exhaust of the small Toyota still unfixed. He could hear the cough of it growing louder through the sporadic rumble of thunder as the late afternoon's threatening storm was about to break.

He rose to a sitting position on the floor beside the trunk, slightly better but still ill; at least the nausea had left him.

Put-put; put-put . . .

What to do? —Confront her; shout like a madman from the top of the stairs as she entered the door dopey from her day's bout with memory and MDA-MMDA: *"Christine—! I've opened your goddamn trunk—!"*

Put-put . . .

He couldn't think. All the pieces of him were lying

scattered throughout nowhere. No; he couldn't do a thing, really nothing yet. There wasn't enough of himself left to act like a self.

Put-put . . .

And then he stood and looked through the round port-hole window of the attic's attic into the blue gloom of the overcast day, the horizon like watered ink, the sky occasionally cracking with streaks of jagged far-off fire.

Where in God's name were the children?—he hadn't seen them for hours. And then, at that very moment, he saw them, sitting in the summerhouse, watching the growing storm, probably starving to death because he had forgotten to give them lunch. Now he saw the Toyota, too, scooting along the white pebbled drive like a black beetle.

It stopped directly below him, clearly within his vision, and as Christine got out the children ran to her. He saw her kneel to kiss Jamie and Rose and then shoo them into the house, each with a small package, probably presents she had brought from the village.

She herself then paused, stood still, facing the black horizon, probably enjoying the threat of the imminent storm, her lightly bandaged hands loosely crossing her chest, a flurry of moths just beginning to gather.

Perhaps she intuited or inexplicably "felt" an invasion of privacy, a disruptive intrusion into the thought or mood that preoccupied her. Whatever the reason, she turned very slowly, and having turned, looked up directly at Michael's face framed in the round, ornate window.

Their eyes met through the vaulted gloom, and as they met, a moth fluttered against the attic screen.

It was like an unexpected slap, an insult so insolent he trembled with rage, then shivered, wanting to shout at the black winged abomination: "Not *me*, stupid! The person you want is down there—*down there!*"

And then, strength temporarily recovered, his hair prickling, his brain rekindled from the ashes of an afternoon that seemed to have charred his life to the marrow of the bone, he wanted to shout at her, too—vulgar, horrid, obscene, ghastly, ridiculous, *awful* things, like: *father fucker! —Palm-holed father fucker! Rotten, L'Enfance du Christ-playing, pseudo-crucified, fake-Christ masturbator! Phoney, dildo-brandishing, self-fucking onanist!*

And however passionate the moment and sad and sick the desire, it was not so passionate and sad and sick that his scholarly if not usually pedantic mind wasn't to the last sufficiently contained and curious to question the grammatical legitimacy of his use of the final epithet, *onanist,* since, considering its etymological source— Onan, who had spent, or was it spilled? his seed upon the ground—it may have applied only to men and never to women.

Christine made no visible movement; there was nothing in her physical attitude to express or reveal surprise or concern that she was looking at him where he was: sanctum sanctorum: in the attic's attic.

All she did finally was smile, and her bandaged hand came up across her face in a friendly wave.

She *knew* what he had done! She *knew* he had opened the trunk and explored its hideous contents! She knew and didn't care! Either it was simply another game she had won, God damn her, or his knowing no longer mattered. Perhaps she was prepared to face him. —Or, rather, *not* to face him; yes—that was clearly it, for her utter lack of concern, her shrugging indifference that would relegate the trunk to boring trivia and make any conversation about it impossible, was only too obvious. No wonder she was able to smile and wave and now, in a display of

final, intolerable conceit, snip off a bit of the last of the
flowering honeysuckle that she might enjoy more intimately its sweet heady scent, while a few more of the
moths, encouraged by the fading light, the deepening
color of the stormy sky, fluttered gracefully around her.

Could he kill her?
Did he want to?
Should he?
Was he able?
Could he take that slender, pale, perfect throat between
his two grimy, clawed hands and smother, strangle, crush
the life from her? Wouldn't it be as easy—or as difficult—as killing, as he had killed, dozens of those maimed
and mutilated starlings? Wasn't *she* as maimed, as muti-
lated—*more* so than those fucking birds, those wretched,
blood-slimed lumps of jumping, mangled, feathered
flesh that he'd had, weepingly, to stomp and squeeze to
death *because of her*?!
Dr. Ellenbogen—Who *is the patient* . . . ?
Thinking about the starlings, Michael began to weep
again . . .
Mr. Kouris—
Tears so watered his eyes that his view of Christine began to waver . . .
You had a mother who, for two years, was insane . . .
. . . Blur and swim . . .
And then killed herself . . .
He wiped his eyes clear.
Dr. Ellenbogen—
Christine waved again, and then, as if everything were
quite *normal*, gestured to the sky, wanting him to enjoy it
with her, see the wild blue-blackness of the clouds that
were beginning to roll and tumble over the top of the
house.

Are all my grievances, complaints, descriptions of events . . . subjective?—part of a phantasy world I myself have created . . . ?

Christine gestured again, indicating that she wanted him to come down.

So you've had reason to think about death, about killing, whether it be the other or self. And what conclusion have you reached . . .?

Christine's hands cupped her mouth as she shouted: "Michael! Come down! Do you hear? The light is *fantastic!* Come look at the sky!"

Dr. Ellenbogen—

Mr. Kouris—

He couldn't go down; not yet. —Even to kill her, if that's what he desired. He wasn't in sufficient control. He was crying again; his legs were weak and wouldn't bear his weight. His hands were shaking, and there was a deep, odd pain in his chest.

Above all, his mind was so sore and aching, so emotionally drained and depleted that, in order to go on living, he had to slide to the floor, in the next few moments, profoundly asleep.

The Departure

He has crowned thy head with flowerets and with laurel, stained thy mouth with lee. How your fangs gleam!

Your breasts are like a lyre through which your androgynous heart beats.

Walk gently through the night, my Love; move that thigh, so!—and then the next: print thy footprint well!

ONE

DR. ELLENBOGEN HAD WHAT SHE'D PERSONALLY
named a "mandala theory" of success or failure, recovery
or demise of the mind.

During work with a patient, if the work was sufficient
and sufficiently inspired, the "design" of the neurosis/
psychosis would finally emerge, and to her tutored, experienced sensibilities, emerge (sometimes while dream-
ing) *visually*—as an abstract or non-objective "picture":
she would see the beginning and growth of its ultimate
"shape" in the form of a mandala, its proportions, colors,
the materials of which it was composed—all the bits and
pieces juxtaposed and fitting together—as if she had in
view the delicate intricacies of a vast mosaic.

It was usually a moment of great discovery and excitement for the doctor because it meant that from that moment on, the work would progress rapidly, coming to a
conclusion in a matter of weeks—either in terms of swift

and complete recovery of the patient or, in rare cases, rapid total surrender to what then had to be considered the insoluble complexities of the neurosis/psychosis.

Regrettably, just as there were some incurable physical diseases that, once established, became rapidly terminal, so with the mind: there were kinds of manifestations of neurosis/psychosis that were indeed terminal and, if they did not literally kill the patient outright, they destroyed the effective ego structure of the personality, confining a selfless mind in a psychic prison that was non-dimensional, that is, beyond the reach of space-time recognitions and therefore totally inaccessible for effective treatment.

Of course, in some cases, if one were so inclined, the irrational behavior and activities of such patients could continue to be observed and studied—even perhaps understood and enjoyed in terms of the imagination, as symbol and metaphor; in a word, as *literature.*

In such unreal, actually *sur*real worlds—of symbol and metaphor, of literature, do autistic children abide. Because of their youth and the relative simplicity of the usually discoverable traumata that converged to create their autism, they are sometimes not inaccessible. With the adult, however, particularly the intelligent and gifted schizophrenic who fashions and *moves into* an independent and unique world, the difficulties are occasionally so compounded that although the mandala appeared to Dr. Ellenbogen after concentrated work and was, as all mandalas must be, bilateral, it was superficial and soon disintegrated into an indecipherable occult pattern. So then, the condition was considered terminal and the demise of the mind only a matter of time.

In Christine's case, the mandala had finally appeared, and was of such astonishingly complex and darkly brilliant composition that it was absolutely thrilling to the doctor. So much so, that she literally danced about the room, her long hair cracking against the furniture like a whip, knocking over a lamp; this she righted with an abashed smile and some embarrassment, since she so seldom surrendered to such extravagant displays of childish emotion.

Still, one must celebrate one's successes, reward oneself for work well done, and Christine's mandala was frankly, if frighteningly, superb.

How unexpected and amazing was the simple, long overlooked discovery that the mere capitalization of an "H" was the master literary motif to Christine's exquisite world of symbol and metaphor: its center *Him*, the black sun of her *living* literature.

The good doctor could barely wait to disclose the news of her success to Michael Kouris, and sat fidgeting with her elaborate recording device, listening to snatches of dialogue, until his unscheduled but requested arrival.

Her housekeeper had left that morning to attend a funeral on the West Coast, and the doctor was alone in the house when the bell rang.

She opened the door to see Michael on crutches, his pale face haggard, his sunken eyes darkly underscored and bright with the gleam of suffering and fear.

She soon learned of his "illness," including the "paralysis" of his legs, and was instantly relieved. The symptoms he exhibited couldn't have been more obviously and simply connected with the items he'd discovered in Christine's trunk, all of which she had just recently "seen" herself on the girl's ES under a massive dose of MDA-MMDA.

"Mr. Kouris—"

She had to say it with an uncharacteristic sigh of sadness and impatience. "It is *so* simple; your symptoms are clearly hysterical and self-punitive.

"What you did—" her black eyes flashing with pleasure "—was to identify with Christine's father when you looked at the photos. After all, Mr. Kouris—*you* and Marcus Damenian *chose the same woman* to love!

"And you, with your suppressed and only partially repressed sexual passion for children (*admit it! admit it! and throw your crutches away!*) must have all but lost your mind in jealousy, desire, and shame, seeing the infant Christine in her father's sexual embrace. It was, *is*, exactly what you would have wanted for yourself! But so intolerable is the admission that now you cannot walk, and are probably totally impotent besides. Mr. Kouris. I am ashamed of you . . . !

"Do you remember when we discussed murder and agreed that we, each of us, is a potential murderer? Given the right circumstances, specific to our natures, we are, all of us, murderers, we said, guilty *before the fact.* So also are we all seducers of children: every father wants to sleep with his daughter, every mother with her son. And sometimes sons with their fathers and daughters with their mothers! And vice versa. What do you think the id does all day long—sit on its hands?

"But fortunately, for culture, for civilization, not to mention good manners, we don't often indulge our murderous, incestuous desires. —But I should not paraphrase Freud quite so illy; I do think I hear his bones groaning a bit in his grave.

"What I would like—since we should get on and discuss my recent discoveries regarding Christine—is for you to think over what I have told you, understand its truth and its simple mechanism, because that's *all* that it is, and then, later on today, perhaps when you leave, or tomorrow at the latest, *throw* your crutches away—and walk! Yes?—Mr. Kouris—?"

However, "Mr. Kouris" didn't walk at all that day, and on the following there was no need to.

When he left Dr. Ellenbogen's office, he still swung his useless, sensationless legs like a human pendulum, back and forth, to and fro, as he went down the steps and out into the street to meet Christine, who had come to pick him up and was waiting for him at the corner, the *put-put* of the Toyota causing annoyed glances from passersby.

"How did it go?" she asked, throwing his crutches into the back seat and helping him into the car.

He didn't answer.

They were about two miles out of town when she asked, more conversationally than wanting to know: "What happened?"

Still no reply.

It was a season of storms, apparently; the sky in the west was blackening again; a few drops of rain splattered against the windshield. Then, in another mile, the darkest of the clouds was directly overhead and a pale sulphurous streak had appeared low on the horizon.

"I think it will pass," Christine murmured.

A sudden violent wind hit the car, a gust that made it swerve a few feet into the left-hand lane.

Christine laughed. "Goodness! Did you feel that!? I wish it were a cyclone. I'd like to be picked up and flung a thousand miles away. —Like Dorothy. —In *The Wizard of Oz*. Wouldn't you like that, Michael?" And she dared steal a glance at the dour and doleful man.

They had almost reached the turnoff to the drive that led to the house when he answered her question from twenty minutes ago.

"What happened *was*," he said, "that I killed Dr. Ellenbogen."

There was no immediate response from Christine, who kept her eyes on the road and her bandaged hands on the wheel to avoid a few well-known potholes.

But presently, after they had cleared the rough spots, she asked: "Why did you do that?"

Murderer, both before and after the fact apparently, Michael was prepared with a private joke that he knew she wouldn't understand, but he said it anyway. "Well—I guess I was 'given the right circumstance, specific to my nature.' "

Christine laughed with pleasure at what to her was nonsense. "Whatever does that mean? You mustn't speak to me in riddles. Not today."

"Why not today?" Michael wanted to know.

The house was in sight, and with it, he thought, surely the end of his life, one way or another, better sooner than later. What was he to do?—go to his study, open a book, resume work on his essay?

"Why not today?" he repeated, insisting on an answer. "Why must I not speak in riddles today?"

"Because—" Christine replied, shrugging as if it were obvious, "—it is a very *special* day."

"*Why* is it special?" Michael pursued, relentlessly.

Christine didn't answer immediately.

"Well, for one thing" she said slyly, making a deliberate moue at his obtuseness, "—for one thing, because you have just *killed* Dr. Ellenbogen."

Michael actually laughed, despite his profound, bewildered, heartaching misery, wondering how in the world he could have been so stupid as to have asked.

He was glad he hadn't told her the rest: how, after he'd struck Dr. Ellenbogen, he'd pulled the tape from her machine and from ten or more spools in her desk—intricate *miles* of it: heaping it over and around the body in tangled profusion—a shining bier that became an instant pyre, the room incandescent the moment, before closing the door, he'd tossed back a match.

TWO

As CLEVER AND EXPERIENCED as she was, Dr. Ellenbogen had not noticed, or, perhaps, in her excitement, simply underestimated the pervasive quality, the soul-drenched depths of Michael Kouris' depression, including his bitterness and rage, the afflux of loathing and hatred that was turned so dangerously inward, against himself.

Seeing the crutches, the dark tortured eyes, the glint of terror lighting them, she should have been able to recognize the immensity of his suffering, and, indeed, offer the help and comfort of which, by nature and profession, she was eminently capable.

Instead, by endowing him with an intelligence and a capacity for self-insight he in no way possessed, and accusing him of being the vicious author and not the victim of his symptoms, she cruelly misjudged him.

To make things worse, her almost instant revelation

confirming the identity of one of his until-now repressed facets of his own sexual nature—*amorinfanticide*—with that of his wife's late father, was the last dreadful twist of the psychic knife.

He had somehow managed to reach the doctor's sound-proof, windowless, ultraprivate office in a remote part of the house, drop his crutches beside him on the floor, and sink into a chair. He declined with a negative wave the glass of brandy offered, but then, not knowing yes from no in his disoriented state, seized it with trembling hands, spilling some of it down his shirtfront, draining the last drop of all that remained.

The doctor had been talking from the moment he entered, with much more animation than was characteristic of her usual modest self. She also played, he was dimly aware, sections of tape, striding theatrically about the room as the machine droned on.

For a while, he watched her with curious detachment, as if she were merely a mime on a stage; he made no effort at all, being incapable of it, to understand what was happening: all of it unintelligible. Only isolated words and phrases from the doctor or the machine flicked like sparks across the short circuit of his mind: something about Christine and mandalas, discoveries, psychosomatic symbolism . . . all of it a remote, vaguely conscious gibberish until a third glass of brandy, which he managed to pour for himself, brought a semblance of life to those intricate areas of his brain that were designed to translate sounds and words into meaning.

" . . . The dream," said an excited but slightly hushed voice, "is *exquisite* architecture"—while two small hands, delicate and as maze-cracked as ancient porcelain, built imaginary gothic steeples in the air. The metaphor was abruptly changed: " . . . a marvelous *lan-*

guage composed of an infinite alphabet of visual and other symbols."

She whirled her body in a dancelike movement, and in doing so, the whip of her long hair, though she didn't realize it, struck Michael rather smartly across the face.

The blow, obviously unintentional, nevertheless so piqued him that his instinct was to strike her back. He had the good sense to refrain.

The curious moment passed, serving further to awaken his senses to listen more attentively to what she was saying, the monologue continuing with measured deliberate speed and, now, just a bit of majesty, the speech apparently *ex cathedra.*

"And if so the dream, what of the phantasy?—the autistic phantasy or, more to our purpose, the schizophrenic phantasy?—in Christine's case, the creation of a whole *other* world, but one so concrete as to vie absolutely with the world you-and-I share, the world *we* call 'reality,' Mr. Kouris."

The whip of her hair as she turned struck him again. Not knowing it, she paused, looking at his tense, outraged expression, demanding: "Why do you look so surprised? You know of what I speak: among so many things, Christine's *hands*, of course. —Truly astonishing. —Thrilling beyond words! And the 'phantom' chauffeur! . . . in his impeccable black livery. Do you realize it, *the children see him, too!* By some incredible act of will, of seduction, she has managed to draw them into the orbit of her phantasy world, made them share it. But Mr. Kouris—I ask—Is that possible? *Can* one *share* a phantasy? Hear this! If *you* see something that no one else sees, you are labeled insane. Correct? But if *I* see it, too, if we *both* see it, *share* it, then it is of course 'real.' Do you understand? So-called 'reality' is nothing more than 'sharing'—a contract, an agreement, so to speak, to see, hear, taste, smell, touch *the same thing*. So then. What kind of strange, shared 'phantasy' are we dealing with here? If Christine and Jamie and Rose *see* the chauffeur, if their experience of him is the same, their descriptions identical, *is* he a phantasy? Impossible! He is *real*, dear sir!—if not of the reality you-and-I know.

"Is he subreal, Mr. Kouris? Superreal? Who's to say, just yet?"

And she smiled her mummy's smile.

"But to finish . . . "

"Most astonishing of all—to me, at least—the one touch that unnerves me, is Christine's control of the moths that will create and clothe her in her bridal gown: *this* is the most breathtaking of all, because, do you see, Mr. Kouris—by some unimaginable chemistry, comparable only perhaps to the digestion of wood pulp by the white ant, she has managed to invade and wrest secret knowledge from one of the darkest and most alien of all worlds: that of the insect.

"She is able to synthesize in her own body and secrete that irresistible female sexual scent that attracts the male *Novabiscum lapustatorium*, the rare, black-winged, hawk-eyed, weaver moth that has been breeding, as you know, by the *thousands*, in the untended areas and wild spaces of your apple orchard!

"Are you ill, Mr. Kouris?"

The doctor's face, inches close to his now, revealed a skin so crazed with minute cracks it looked like an enameled mask taken from a kiln a month too late.

"I mean—" she added, gesturing to his crutches and the "paralysis" that apparently extended from his waist down, rendering his legs useless "—beyond this!—your obvious illness."

"No . . . " The word was hoarse, barely a whisper.

"But you seem faint, and so very pale. You're not, somehow, yourself today. I wouldn't have called you, I needn't have insisted on your being here at all, except—"

"Yes?"

"Well, my news was so stimulating . . . "

She smiled again, more broadly now, and he half-expected the skin to crack into flakes that would fall to his lap in a shower of pink and white confetti.

" . . . Christine and I made so much progress so quickly. I thought it would be really good for you to know. As I've told you so often, schizophrenia never strikes *one* without striking another, sometimes many others. . . . It is a disease of relationships, and—"

The doctor paused, still puzzled by his appearance, his remote, unheeding manner and behavior.

"Mr. Kouris—"

Michael desired to cross his legs, since, sensationless, ostensibly "dead," they had separated slowly and spread themselves wide, looking positively obscene. To cross them, however, he had to lift one with both hands and fling it over the other.

"Mr. Kouris— Actually, I have little more to say at the moment. I think I have brought you up to date. So perhaps it would be best . . . "

Michael understood and slowly reached for his crutches. With one on his lap, he hesitated, raising a hand inquiringly.

"Before I go . . . "

"Yes."

"One thing I don't understand . . . "

"Yes?"

" . . . is why you mentioned . . . "

"Yes?"

" . . . Christine's . . . "

She waited.

" . . . *bridal* gown."

The doctor couldn't have been more surprised. She stepped back, prepared to sit down again.

"Christine is *betrothed.*"

The stupid, glazed look on the man's face remained.

"Mr. Kouris— Betrothed *psychologically*—schizophre nically, if you will; in the strange *real-unreal* world we just discussed."

"But—?"

"Yes?"

"—To *whom?*"

The doctor threw up her hands, falling back into her chair.

"*Where* have you been? In your *own* phantasy world! Have I been talking to my walls for two hours, playing my machine to myself when I have heard it a thousand times before? Mr. Kouris— Your wife is betrothed to *Him—to Him.*"

Michael flushed, never before having been subject to the doctor's impatience.

"To . . . him?" he questioned faintly.

Dr. Ellenbogen put a hand to one ear, leaning toward him, listening intently as she made him repeat the word; then, unsure, she asked: "Are you using a capital?"

"I beg your pardon?"

"Is your *Him* capitalized, Mr. Kouris? Are you using a *capital* 'H'?"

It was obvious he hadn't understood and probably never would; he had deceived her for hours, mostly with his silence, but also with his little nods and smiles and swallows of brandy, so she angrily ripped a page from a notebook and wrote the word down in big sprawling letters, thrusting it at him.

"There—do you see!—a capital 'H' . . . *Him!*"

Michael held the scrap of paper in trembling hands, feeling that his IQ of 145 must have slipped down to 20.

"But . . . I mean . . . That is to say . . . "—the paper fluttering— ". . . a capital usually implies a deity. Are we to assume something religious? Does she . . . does Christine imagine, as some women do—in nunneries, I believe—that she is *betrothed* to Christ, so to speak?"

Dr. Ellenbogen moved back in her chair, weary, discouraged, but resigned to repeating herself.

"I think not," she replied evenly.

"Then what *do* you think? Who *is* he? I mean *He*? I mean *Him*?"

"Mr. Kouris—" She sighed. "I know many things. But perhaps not all. To digress just a moment—I remember the time when psychoanalysis was popular, and people were forever saying, 'Freud *said this* . . . ' and 'Freud *said that* . . . ' Actually, Freud never said very much at all. His genius was to *convey* what he had learned from his patients. Consequently, it would have been *correct* to say, 'Freud's *patients* said this . . . Freud's *patients* told him that . . . '"

She paused. "And that is what I say to you. If *He* has a name, Christine did not tell me what it was, or is, though I do know that at one time she mentioned the legend of Faust. Does that help at all?" She laughed, momentarily pleased with her own bit of teasing. "In my own case, I am inclined toward 'Principality,' but in the sense of an exquisite personification of 'evil,' though I must add that I am truly happiest with the pronoun; it will most certainly do, and I don't wish to vulgarize it with popular and inadequate nomenclature."

While she talked, she pressed buttons and twisted the

various dials of her elaborate tape machine; there was a sound as if a heavy casette had dropped into place. Above a faint whirring noise, she continued:

"So you see, your assumption is not correct. Christine is not betrothed to Christ. Think of the stigmata. The wounds imply that she is *identified* with Christ. She *is* the Nazarene. She is a *feminized* Christ."

There was no surprise, no delight, no wonder at all on Michael Kouris' face. Only blankness and stupidity.

"You ask *why?*" the doctor supplied, putting words in his mouth, anxious to conclude. "I answer: how could it be otherwise? *He* has His work in the world, has He not? And if you'll forgive my admiration, how splendid! To *feminize* Christ; 'Good' becomes *passive, open, receptive*; 'Evil' *active, mobile, penetrating*. Mr. Kouris—if there's a Groom, there must be a Bride. Prepare yourself for a Wedding of Darkness and Light."

"I knew I was betrothed," said a voice from the machine, "when I was a child. Very young. My father told me many times, in great detail. But to a child, I think it must have seemed a story; I know I asked to hear it again and again, as children do."

"That's not my wife's voice," Michael said.

"But then, after a while, I somehow forgot—that I was betrothed, I mean, though I sometimes dreamt about it. I dreamt of *Him,* too, His great beauty and sexual mystery, how strange He was!—always in shadow, with an essential darkness about Him, as well as everything that surrounded Him.

"And do you know: the people who were always with Him—and the variety of other creatures: birds, insects, angels, too—I could see those plainly—always seemed able to fly. Everyone, most everything, had wings! It was somehow necessary, or at least greatly desirable.

"I used to dream of having wings myself: graceful, but immensely strong, with fine sturdy bones and hard muscle growing them from my back. The shoulder blades, if you do not know it, are vestigial wings. And I have heard, though it happened more frequently in ancient times, that even today some babies are born with tiny, malformed wings behind their shoulders, the same as some babies are born with small, bony tails extending from the vertebrae, growing outside the body at the end of the spine.

"Of course, the doctors who deliver such babies, and their parents, too, are terribly alarmed and disturbed, even embarrassed at the brilliance of such a birth, considering it an anomaly; consequently, they order the wings or the tails cut off instantly. But if you were to consult the physical education or hygiene departments of many elementary schools, you will soon enough find in their files records of children who have small scars on their shoulder blades and the anal tips of their spines . . . "

"That is not my wife's voice," Michael said.

"So you see, for this reason, there are no longer winged angels in the ordinary, visible world, only in private worlds. Otherwise, to appear at all, and not be killed on sight, they must take other and occult forms, such as extraordinary birds or bizarre insects. Sometimes one will appear *collectively*: that is, in the guise of a vast metropolis of one of the so-called 'social' insects. Once, in Africa, I remember seeing a gigantic termite mound, at least a hundred feet high, that contained an angel.

"In any event, soon I virtually forgot the story that my father had told me—of my betrothal, and dreamt of it less and less, though I always, *always* expected, just below the threshold of consciousness, that *some*thing extraordinary would happen in my life. That I knew. Just as I knew that I had to prepare—with Jamie and Rose, which I did, of course. But even after they were born, there were so many years to wait, and so much ordinary living to do . . . "

"But—" It was the doctor's voice interrupting the other which sounded so uncannily like Christine's. "I don't understand something—quite. You were betrothed, yes; but by *whom?*"

Laughter: happy, delighted, like a child's.

"By my *father*, of course!" Ridiculing—"By *whom!*"

Silence.

An odd drumming: the doctor's fingers, perhaps; pale lacquered nails gently tapping against the shiny surface of her desk.

"But—" The doctor again, pausing to clear her throat, audibly swallowing, so fine was the machine's reception.

"But—*why?*"

More laughter.

"Because . . . I've *told* you . . . he *adored* Him. No one could have loved Him more. My father would have done anything . . . *any*thing . . ."

"Even—"

" . . . *anything* to please Him."

"—even . . . to giving a child, a daughter, and grand-children not yet born?"

"That is *not*," Michael shouted, outraged by the deception, seizing the crutch on his lap, "Christine's voice!"

But of course, it was. And from the machine: answering the doctor's final question: delight unbounded, laughter gentle now, sublime.

"—Oh!—that was the *least!* I *told* you: my father *adored* Him—beyond time, beyond death, beyond all the recognitions . . . asking nothing, fulfilling all in his power. I was . . . I *am* . . . the *least* of the least . . .

The smallest, the most trivial of gifts . . . the most incidental of flatteries. You must know He enjoys being flat-
tered and made much of! Hasn't He always? Hear me: I
was *made* for Him . . . ! "

The blow was meant for Christine. Or perhaps her father, Marcus Damenian, in lieu of hammer and stake,
fifty years too late.

But it was the doctor who got it, on the left side just
over and behind the ear with the heavy, armpit end of the
crutch, shattering a third of her skull without a drop of
blood, the whole area crumpling and folding in like the
crushed dent in a car fender, or as if her head had im-
ploded.

She fell soundlessly: snow upon snow, and with re-
markable grace, knowing quite how to die—even die
unexpectedly: her legs together and modest, the arms by
her sides—not like most wanton corpses, with limbs careless and lewdly postured.

Either it was Michael's dim-witted brain that, now in
shock, was catching time later than it was—as if the
events in the world were out of sync with his mind—or
she fell in slow motion. Either way, it was a ballet under
water: her shining hair fluid, fanning out into loose rolling scrolls as she hit, first the machine, somehow turning
it off, and then the floor. Her body arched upward for a
few seconds, as if God desired to pull her to heaven by
the breastbone, then settled back as limp-limbed as
Christ in the Pieta.

Virtually covered with the shroud of her own beautiful
hair, she could be no one, Michael mused, staring at her
sadly, except the mermaid in Wilde's *The Fisherman and
His Soul*—having left the sea and therefore aged and
grown ancient, but with a half-smile on her withered lips

more teasing and haunting than La Gioconda's itself.
Surely she had known *all* the secrets, he thought, all
the secrets in the world worth knowing.

Except one.

She hadn't known that he would kill her. As he would
soon, most probably, kill Christine.

The storm had passed, barely wetting the ground, but
left the late afternoon sky gloomy and dark, the horizon
massed with blue-black clouds except for the remaining
streak of sulphurous ochre and yellow.

The car was in front of the house; Christine had shut
off the motor, and they were sitting there silently, Michael perfectly motionless and with no expression except
a gathering of deep creases above the bridge of his nose,
and eyes that were truly pathetic with grief and bewilderment.

Why should he be taking the doctor's death quite so se-
riously? It was a mystery to Christine. After having joked
about its being a "special day" to make him laugh—
which he had—she thought the whole thing would be
forgotten, but obviously he was going to be morose and
difficult for the rest of the day.

Actually, it *was* a special day, but not for Michael's reasons: something had been gnawing at her since this
morning—ever since the children's disappearance, long
before she had driven Michael to see the doctor and fretted away more than two hours on her knitting while she
waited.

She tried to isolate her feeling and give it a name. The
doctor probably would have called it another of her
"floating anxiety" attacks, but there was no doctor any
more to call it that, or anything else. So she decided to
name it herself. It was a *"crisis* anxiety"—that sounded

professional, and in a way quite accurate. A crisis was imminent: only hours, perhaps minutes away. *That* was her feeling, which accounted for her nagging anticipation, her sharp-edged expectancy.

Should she be *doing* something, she wondered, to prepare? But she could think of nothing, not knowing at all what the crisis would be.

Poor Michael! Still staring, motionless, his brow furrowed, his eyes so haunted and filled with pain! She could at least try to cheer him up, and her mind raced for possible costumes to wear, dramas he hadn't seen too often to be amused; perhaps a fragment of a *new* play. But what? *What?* Why was her mind so empty today? She remembered the Egyptian-baby play she had never performed—because of those dreadful birds—and she *had* rehearsed it. Dare she attempt to repeat it now? It would be new to Michael. But might he remember the painted pillow he'd found, with its funny drawn face? Would that spoil it?

Her head was beginning to ache—thinking all these thoughts! And her palms throbbed. So many decisions!

So she decided to take one at a time. "Why don't we," she said to Michael, handing him his crutches, "go to the summerhouse for a while? It's cool there, and pleasant. I'll bring you something delicious to eat. You must be hungry. I remember—I always used to be *ravenous* after talking to the doctor; or perhaps it was the drugs she gave me; drugs make you *very* hungry, you know."

Michael had absolutely nothing to say, and did exactly what she told him to do, though he trembled and shook, and had trouble weaving and stumbling toward the summerhouse.

She took the light car robe with them, and when he was seated comfortably, she tucked it snugly around him.

"*There* now!" she said, which was something one always said when one did something especially nice for someone else. She put his crutches on the floor, and her knitting on his lap so at least he'd have something pleasant to look at and soft to touch.

"I wonder . . . " she murmured, and paused, brushing a lock of hair from his forehead. "Perhaps tomorrow, if you're not better, we could inquire about a wheelchair. They do have lovely ones, you know, with electric batteries and all sorts of buttons to push on the handles."

Then she told him about the children, that they'd been missing all day, adding, before she left to bring the food: "Be careful of the knitting needles; I don't want to drop a stitch."

THREE

Christine returned with a saucer full of wild flower honey and a white-enameled colander filled to the rim with chilled strawberries.

She showed Michael how to hold a strawberry by the stem, dip it into the honey, and then quickly, lest it drip, bite into it, the teeth coming down carefully between the tiny cluster of green leaves at the end of the stem and the berry itself.

"My father taught me that," she said. "Did we ever do it before?"

She stared at him, disappointed. He hadn't moved, and his face was still so dark and bitter and stony.

"Oh, Michael! *Do* try some; they're delicious. I *know* you'll like them!"

He did try one, his hand shaking, but he was like a tiny baby on solid food for the first time, the mashed, half-chewed fruit all over his mouth and chin.

"Oh, Michael!" And she had to clean him off.

She couldn't understand why he didn't speak, and his bewildered eyes which kept staring into hers and seemed to be trying to *say* something that words couldn't. What? *What?*

When he wasn't looking at her, his eyes kept roving to the apple orchard, the house, the grounds, perhaps looking for the children.

So she said again what she'd said before, hoping it would help.

"Michael, I've looked *every*where. And I've shouted myself hoarse. They're simply *no*where. But you mustn't worry. They've gone away before; you know that. Of course, not for *this* long—never for a whole day. But they're only hiding: it's one of their silly games. They'll be back, I'm sure. Children their age don't disappear." She laughed. "There are no wild *gypsies* to steal them, and they're much too young to run away."

But there was no cheering him up, and his gloom, not Christine's good spirits, became infectious.

She tried to knit, but her hands were hurting too much. What *was* the matter with them today!?

The novelty of the wounds had worn off weeks ago; they were a nuisance and a bore. And so hot and throbbing under the bandages she couldn't bear the pain. Perhaps some cool fresh air . . . And she began unwinding them slowly.

She stopped midway, because Michael had jolted in his seat, watching her. Evidently he didn't want to *see* her hands, possibly because they were so unpleasant. Well, that was just too bad. They were *her* hands, not his, and they hurt.

The bandages came off, and the cool air on the surface

of the open bloodless wounds *did* feel better. She glanced at Michael, but his eyes were downcast, his head averted.

She looked more closely at her hands, then held them above her head that she might look through the open tear-shaped holes at the sky.

As she did so, the wounds turned crimson. She lowered her hands and dropped them, palm-upward in her lap, watching a slow welling of blood, brighter than the brightest strawberry at her side, fill in the wounds until they looked like tiny pools, then, as the blood swelled, rounded upward and hardened, like rubies. And like rubies they remained.

A single moth drifted by, gliding around Christine's head in wide, but diminishing circles. It was the largest, the darkest, the most beautiful of any of the thousands she had seen, and alighted surprisingly, on her left shoulder, facing her, its wings flattened and still. The creature's lack of shyness and fear, its display of pride and, yes, conceit! amused her, and, smiling, she turned her head slowly to find herself staring deeply into two golden, fractured eyes.

Michael's eyes were neither fractured nor golden; they were their usual if now glassy blue—but aghast. At what, Christine could only guess. —The insolent gesture of the moth? —The two rubies glittering in her palms? No; his head was turned to one side, his chin lifted. *He was listening.* She turned her own curious eyes to follow the direction of his gaze. What had he heard?

The children!? Were they back? Had they returned?

The children *hadn't* returned. They never would.

What Michael had heard, of course—even, astonishingly before Christine—was the crunch of pebbles in the driveway.

The magnificent car, gleaming black with glints of gold, moved in the continued slow motion of Michael's mind, nosing from out of the gloom between the arched wet foliage that lined either side of the drive in the distance where an accumulation of fog was weaving and threading itself from branch to branch, from tree to tree, like the cobwebs across the windows of an ancient house.

The car seemed to creep rather than roll, its immense weight crushing the stones so steadily it became a faint roar, though as usual occasionally a few loose pebbles were caught by the tire treads and spun up, rattling under the fenders.

In the many minutes it took to move the length of the drive and stop abreast of the summerhouse only a few yards away, nothing else in the world existed for both Michael and Christine. They could see the Driver at the wheel, and both knew, each in his own way, the import of His coming.

For obscure reasons, Michael desired to stand, to be on his feet when the Chauffeur stepped from the car. He groped blindly for his crutches, never, for one second, allowing his eyes to stray from the car. His paralysis, however, had affected more than his legs: his left arm was difficult, almost impossible to move, and along with it, he felt a numbed, dead sagging of muscles and tissue on the left side of his face. So while he groped and twisted, making faint, fearful grunting noises and clattering the one crutch he had managed to reach, the feat was impossible; he couldn't stand, and fell back, half-inclined, half-collapsed to the floor of the summerhouse, the entire left half of his body having died.

As the Chauffeur stepped from the car on the driver's side, moving around as usual to open the rear door on the right, Michael could see Christine stand, and, of all things, remove everything she wore, even her shoes!

Her nakedness, however, was virtually instantaneous, for a fantastic cloud of wings immediately descended, clothing her, wrist to throat, throat to ankle, in the lightest most weightless of silks, the richest and darkest of velvets: all of it breathing, living, alive: obedient, superbly accommodating to every gesture, every subtle movement of her body: ever ready to fold, to separate, to billow, scroll, twist, waft, float, cling.

The Chauffeur seemed pleased, a smile turning up the corners of His handsome mouth, but He seemed also touched with a faint anxiety, the lips parting in questioning anticipation.

Was it *still* not time? Was something *more* required, some . . . final gesture?

Christine knew what it was, and turned both of her palms toward him, exposing the two bright jewels. Seeing them, the Chauffeur's smile became wide, His eyes crinkling with pleasure.

Perhaps Christine *walked* to the car, but to Michael's one remaining eye she appeared to levitate, perhaps only a quarter-inch or so from the ground, but that was all that was needed to make her glide effortlessly, to float.

Michael

He spoke to his friends of revelations, of trials ter-
minated. They leaned on each other in ecstasies,
while tapestries were hung from all the houses.

ONE

THERE WERE MOMENTS NOW, after an incredible swift, short journey that seemed more by air than by road, when Christine had no idea where she was or what she was doing.

Was she lying on Dr. Ellenbogen's couch in the throes of a massive dose of MDA-MMDA?—a mistaken overdose that had brought on a dangerous, perhaps even fatal convulsion?

Was she dying? Was Michael *killing* her?—finally, inevitably, as she knew he would; or were the twin white blurs she saw a double vision of the doctor's panicked face? Were the hands that seized her, crushed her, trying to drag her back into life? Was the breath that she breathed not her own, but mouth-to-mouth from another?

But she was going so fast, she was far ahead of herself, and made a violent, strained effort to go back, to order time so she could experience now as *now* and real as *real*.

Obedient to her will, time apparently righted itself; at least a reality of a kind ebbed back.

Was she attending a festival, a masquerade, a fantastic carnival, wedding, or Mardi Gras? Was it Easter morning in Rome, at St. Peter's Square, she standing like a Queen overlooking the half-million or more who knelt silently before her, their heads reverently bowed?

Ah, no; surely it was a bazaar!—a marketplace of shadows among countless acres of decayed buildings where ancient words on crumbling cornerstones and over doorways were now illegible—with awnings by the thousand at all levels in the endless arched reaches of the air, warped canvases of every size and brilliant color, elevated on painted poles of various thicknesses and strung together with knotted rages—a place without buyers or sellers, or indeed merchandise at all, for everything had already been bought and sold; only the flux and flood of the crowd remained, milling throngs of courtly men and beautiful women, elaborately dressed, mixed with performers and entertainers, some gilded, romping everywhere.

Near her, Christine saw an immense cage filled with wild albino monkeys, each with pink eyes and filed teeth, and a great black muzzled bear.

Child to the last, her first thought was: "What a bizarre bazaar!"—laughing at her own absurd joke, clapping her hands until, behind her, He whispered her name.

She heard Him, and turned slowly, seeing her own white face doubled in the twin mirrors of his glasses; then, through the smoky haze she saw Him and knew who He was.

Her smile broadened and deepened, the happiness she

felt bringing a glow to her body, as if a lamp inside had
been lighted.

So enormous, so crushing was the pain and pressure
that seized her, so total and absolute the crowding engine
that entered her, that she thought surely it was the loose
giant bear, while the uncaged monkeys ate ravenously
through the moths to her flesh.

Ravished, impaled, gored in immense bloody issue to
the very heart, She expired, sighing in His arms.

Him

To be sure, floats covered with animals of gilded wood, poles and awnings in motley stripes, embossed and decorated with flags and flowers; coaches filled with naked children, drugged and laughing. Even coffins under dark canopies, lifting aloft their ebony plumes to the trot of huge mares, blue and black.

ONE

HE COULD NEITHER SPEAK NOR CALL OUT, and in the absence of neighbors, anyone who might see him, even of the milkman, whom he heard early one morning rumbling his bottles, unseen, on the back stoop, Michael, only his right side mobile, took three days to reach the house, crawl to a doorway and open it, and another full day, sometimes losing consciousness for hours at a time, to move to his study where he had hidden Christine's shotgun and what remained of the shells.

It was enormously difficult to load it, but between one good hand and his teeth, he succeeded, and then spent another four hours positioning his body properly, half-sitting, half-lying in a chair, so that what he desired could occur.

He managed it finally: his body arranged: the butt end of the gun wedged against his dead foot, the long double-barrel extending upward, a dead left arm wrapped ingeniously around it, holding it squarely in place, the rusted, wide, twin openings sucked into his mouth, bulging both cheeks.

Dr. Ellenbogen— Who *is the patient* . . . ?

And there he sat, for he had to rest a while gathering strength, his breath whistling and rasping through the double mouthful of metal it held; his clothes in rags, half torn from his body in its stupendous crawl from the summerhouse, ruddy with scratches, stained with dried blood, smeared, splattered, grimy with soil and dirt; no longer a man; not even a scarecrow!—for a sparrow, hopping through the door he'd left open, found him making love to his gun, and had the impudence to sit for a while on one of his dead fingers, a shiny bead of an eye blinking at him curiously.

Are all my grievances, complaints, descriptions of events—horrors! griefs! calamities!—subjective? . . . part of a phantasy world I myself have created . . . ? Am I going, have I gone, the the way my mother went?

Michael's heart rushed out toward the bird in an overwhelming desire to embrace it: for, alert, alive, so pert, so becoming, so audacious, it belonged in all its beauty to God; it was God sitting on his finger.

When the bird winged away, Michael's heart went with it, leaving just enough strength in his right forefinger to tighten on the trigger and explode his brain.

TWO

THERE WAS AN INVESTIGATION, of course. In fact, it went on for several years, for although Michael Kouris had obviously killed himself—the evidence of suicide abounding—there were a few suspicious souls who spoke of murder.

After all, his wife was missing and was never heard of again, as well as his two small children. What had happened to *them*?

A morbid and romantic few imagined that—mad as he surely was—Michael Kouris had murdered them all and buried them in the apple orchard, or hidden them somewhere in that vast and hideous house.

But the gossip died down, along with the interest of the investigators.

It was assumed, finally, that Christine Kouris, who was known to have odd ways, had run off with another man. And taken her children and all her belongings with her.

She must have.

Something like that must have happened.

SECOND CHANCE PRESS, Sagaponack, New York 11962

All titles come in $15.95 cloth editions and $7.95 trade paper editions unless otherwise noted.

Bloom, Harry. TRANSVAAL EPISODE. "Fiery and admirable, with power, passion and a controlled savagery that makes it uncomfortable but fascinating reading." *London Daily Telegraph.*

Broun, Heywood Hale. A STUDIED MADNESS. "The most ruefully articulate, inside book on the American Theater in years." *John Barkham.* "A highly entertaining memoir that could be mistaken for a novel." *Milwaukee Journal.*

Conrad, Earl. GULF STREAM NORTH. "A graphic recounting of five days at sea. The crew is black, the captain white, but all are bound together in the mystique and commerce of fishing. A first class reissue." *San Diego Union.*

Degenhard, William. THE REGULATORS. "This six hundred page novel to end all novels about Dan Shays will not let you down. In manages to endow the uprising known as Shays Rebellion with all the sweep of a minor epic." *New York Times.*   (cloth) ... $22.50   (paper) ... $11.95

deJong, Dola. THE FIELD. "An overwhelming tragedy of refugees escaping Europe during World War II, this novel can tell us more about history than do books of history themselves." *St. Louis Globe Democrat.*

Goodman, Mitchell. THE END OF IT. "A classic of American literature; the single American masterpiece about the Second World War." *The Nation* "Philosophical, poetic, it says something new about war." *Norman Mailer.*

Levy, Alan. SO MANY HEROES. "Alan Levy lived through the Russian-led invasion of Czechoslovakia in 1968 and has written about it with an intimacy of detail and emotion that transcends mere journalistic reporting. A large book about a tiny nation's hope and tragedy." *Newsweek.*

Lortz, Richard. LOVERS LIVING, LOVERS DEAD. "The sort of subtle menace last evinced in Henry James' *The Turn of the Screw.* This portrait of innocence corrupted should keep a vast readership in its terrifying grasp." *San Diego Union.*

Lortz, Richard. THE VALDEPEÑAS. "The story begins with a seemingly realistic depiction of a group of vacationers summering off the coast of Spain . . . then becomes progressively surrealistic. Suspense builds to a chaotic ending making this a one-sitting, hard-to-put-down book." *Library Journal.*

O'Neal, Charles. THREE WISHES FOR JAMIE. "A humorous, sensitive love story with adventure, laughter, tears and a sprinkling of Irish folklore." *Los Angeles Times.*

Salas, Floyd. TATTOO THE WICKED CROSS. "An extraordinarily evocative novel set on a California Juvenile prison farm. One of the best and most important first novels published during the last ten years." *Saturday Review.*

Schuman, Julian. CHINA: AN UNCENSORED LOOK. "It is appropriate, timely and fortunate for those who wish to know how it was in China during the momentous years from 1948 through 1953 that the *Second Chance Press* has reprinted this book. Its time has come." *Foreign Service Journal.*

Shepard, Martin. FRITZ. The definitive biography of the founder of Gestalt Therapy. "A masterful yet loving portrait that goes far beyond biography, offering a Fritz Perls to whom few, if any, were privy." *Psychology Today.*

Singer, Loren: THE PARALLAX VIEW. "A tidy, taut and stylish thriller that functions as a political chiller as well! Breathbating suspense." *New York Magazine.*

Stern, Richard: "A brilliant fusing of the themes of a father's attempt to understand and exonerate his son with a plot of wartime espionage." *Richard Ellmann* "Brilliant . . . authentic . . . exciting." *Commonweal.*